THE

WEREWOLVES

OF WINTER

THE ACCURSED NORTH #1

THE WEREWOLVES OF WINTER

Published by Damn Fool Press
www.damnfoolpress.com

Cover illustration is a public domain image from U.S. Centers for Disease Control and Prevention—Medical Illustrator.

ISBN 978-0-9950434-0-4 epub
ISBN 978-0-9950434-1-1 mobi
ISBN 978-0-9936983-9-2 pdf
ISBN 978-0-9936983-8-5 trade paperback

First Edition : November 2016

This is for Lynn and the cats.

CHAPTER ONE
Wash Away Our Sins

Although it was almost noon, the dark clouds and heavy rain made it seem more like late evening. A fitting background for my escape from the legions of werewolves that had attacked and overrun my town, my neighbours—and all too nearly myself.

I've always enjoyed a good rainstorm, and this one was especially welcome. I couldn't afford tears right now, so it was nice of Nature to do the crying for me. Not that I had any tears left to shed.

A slimy glob of something red and sticky flew off the snowplow and smacked against the windshield. The wipers, assisted by the rain, gradually cleaned it off. Until it was gone, a fluid haze of red covered the screen. Werewolf red. Red in tooth and claw.

I took my foot off the accelerator and allowed myself a brief moment to wipe at my face. I was so tired. Tired in body and spirit. I wanted nothing more than to pull over to the side of the highway and stand in the rain, letting it wash me clean.

Alas, rest was for the innocent or the dead. I was neither, so I brought the pickup back up to highway speed and continued my journey down Highway 400 to Toronto. Into the Big Smoke that I had left years ago.

The rain had by this time covered the road with a layer of water, which was now spraying onto the snowplow. It would be nice to get it clean again. I've always hated to leave my tools dirty. Unfortunately, as the plow was cleaned the windshield was sprayed with a mist of blood-soaked water and the odd bit of semi-solid matter.

As I drove, though, there was a gradual lessening of the amount of ick thrown up onto the windshield. The rain was washing away the traces of the horror—at least off the pickup.

The werewolves had been around for years, and the world had adapted. Then everything changed last week. God! Had it only been a week? Yeah, as hard as it was to imagine, that would be about right. I'd set out from my farm to check up on my neighbours. I should have realized the danger then. Maybe been able to do something. Maybe save someone other than just myself.

Maybe.

If only.

CHAPTER TWO
Scouting Trip

I could hear them howling, hunting something or other. Hopefully not someone.

Howling or no, I had wanted to check up on my neighbours. The power, land-line phone, cell phone, and Internet had all been down for over a month, and I'd not heard from any of them in all that time. The signal lights I'd convinced them to rig up over a year ago indicated that everything was OK. Still, it was past time to check up on them all—werewolves be damned--so I had kitted up my truck for the short trip to my neighbours.

The werewolves had begun to leave me alone these days. The beds of garlic, onions, and wolfsbane that I'd planted around the house helped. It didn't seem to do them any real harm, but hives, massive sneezing fits, and tearing eyes could be painful enough to be a useful deterrent.

My shotguns and rifles also encouraged them to stay away from the house. Enhanced healing was of little use when the blast of a 12-gauge shell filled with No. 4 buck hit them in the head or chest. A solid one-ounce slug or the bullet from a .303 worked well, too, although that required more precision when aiming.

So a truce, of sorts, held. Or maybe just a temporary cessation of hostilities. Whatever. They stopped attacking me, and I stopped shooting at them. I wasn't the best of shots, but thankfully the noise of the guns was usually sufficient to chase them off. Circumstances, however, had been forcing me to improve my aim. There were more of them than was normal for this time of year, so I had made a point of practising as much as my limited stock of ammunition allowed.

Alas, the truce, or whatever it was, only seemed to hold within the limits of my yard. As I drove down the road, I would sometimes catch sight of werewolves in the fields or brush. A few darted out to run alongside me for a few seconds before dashing off. Most lay or stood motionless, staring hard at me as I passed.

The back of my neck began to prickle as I began to wonder what would happen if I ever stopped. Or if something made me stop. Now that was an unsettling thought. Not a pleasant drive.

The looks in the eyes of the gathering werewolves was beginning to worry me. I'd seen them dash across the road ahead and behind me. Not often, and not too closely, although it seemed to be happening somewhat more frequently and a bit closer each time.

I caught sight of a couple of larger groups up ahead, trying to blend in with the scrubby spring grasses. That wasn't normal behaviour—small hunting packs were one thing, but this looked like an attempt at an ambush. At the first widening of the road I turned around and headed back home. Although the need to get back home almost made me stomp on the accelerator, I forced myself to keep the speed constant. It was important not to speed up or slow down too much or too quickly. Changes in speed seemed to trigger their hunting reflex, just like it would for any predator.

Sweat was beginning to trickle down my neck as I caught sight of my driveway up ahead. A look around showed nothing out of the ordinary as I made the turn into the driveway and drove towards the house. I glanced at the house and barn and saw that none of the alert lights were on. A good sign, but not foolproof. All that meant was that the motion detectors hadn't sensed anything recently.

The day was too warm for the thermal detectors to be of use, so those weren't going to be of any help. I drove behind the house, and up to the barn. Stopping just outside the garage door, I kept the engine running. The werewolves had learnt the hard way not to rush me at this point. Still, it was always best not to take chances.

I flicked a switch on the pickup's dashboard to arm the active defences, then another to increase the sensitivity of the sensors. Finally the third switch: the AHBL—All Hell Breaking Loose—switch. Sirens warbled and high-intensity LED lights strobed briefly. After a short pause, a different pattern of shrieks and flashes again cycled. With the sensors still showing that all was clear, I disabled the AHBL, and signalled the garage doors to open. At the first opportunity, I drove in and closed the door. Another check of the sensors showed that everything checked out OK.

Home sweet home.

With a heavy sigh of defeat I got out of the truck. There was no point in topping up the fuel tank, given that I'd not gone very far. On the other hand, adding some more gasoline stabilizer couldn't hurt. I was old enough to remember when gasoline could sit for practically ever and still be usable. With all the newfangled "enhancements" and "eco-friendly additives", gasoline now started to degrade within a week or two. I grabbed a bottle of stabilizer gunk and poured it into the gas tank. There was a limited supply of the gunk that I figured would run out at about the same time the gasoline did. Hard decisions were coming up later in the year. Another heavy sigh as I replaced the cap on the fuel tank and shut the lid.

With the vehicle's needs taken care of, I removed the emergency duffel bag and guns and stowed them in their appropriate storage locations. I turned to check the upper floor, then with a start remembered that I had yet to lock the garage door.

"Absent-minded old fool," I muttered under my breath.

Turning towards the garage door, I slid the locking bolts on both sides—top, middle, and bottom bolts. Yes, the garage door opener mechanism was supposed to protect the door from brute force attacks. However, when my life was on the line I preferred to err on the side of caution.

That chore completed, I continued into the barn proper. I

had turned it into a general-purpose workshop and vehicle storage building shortly after moving here, some years ago. The bottom floor had about one third of it devoted to vehicles—the pickup, a medium-sized tractor, and a couple of snow blowers. The remaining space held small and medium-sized CNC mills and lathes for metal work, a laser cutter, a woodworking lathe, a small CNC mill for general wood carving, and a large CNC mill suitable for carving up full sheets of plywood. The finishing areas that had been used for painting and such, were now converted to storage and supplemental backup power.

Upstairs, where I was heading, was more or less office space. Once packed with computers and electronic gizmos, now it was a main hub for sensors and security. The uppermost loft also made a good sniper blind, with a field of view that stretched as far as several of my nearest neighbours.

I wearily climbed the stairs. This seemed to be getting harder every month. Much of that was just psychological, I knew. Not entirely, though—the advancing years seemed to take their toll, no matter how much I tried to outwit or deny them.

Reaching the top of the stairs, I headed over to the security system. It showed no untoward activity, and I decided to take advantage of that to start running a diagnostic. Although the system ran a diagnostic automatically every twenty-four hours, it never hurt to run them more often. Some of the sensors communicated via WiFi, some via cables running into serial ports, and some plugged into a hardwired network using CAT6 cable. A mixed bag of technologies that had evolved over the years and changed as technology changed. Now it was frozen into an as-is state, and as such it was a damn fine idea to run diagnostics to catch any issues or potential issues as quickly as possible.

It was too early for the thermal scanners to be of use, so there was no data from them. The motion sensors showed the usual random movements caused by wind, movement of the trees, and birds. I truly loathed the motion sensors, as they gave so many false positives. Still, once in a while they picked up something that the other sensors missed. Often enough that I didn't begrudge them the power it took to keep them working, nor the time spent in analysing their data. That didn't stop them from being an annoying pain in the ass much of the time. The video feeds were little better. Image analysis software was useful—although, like the motion sensors, it was prone to false positives.

Open source software was a god-send in setting this all up. However, with a workforce of one to do the programming, cooking, cleaning, security, and everything, well, it was hard to find the time to do it all properly. And, if truth be told, I wasn't the world's best techie. Talented enough to do some useful stuff, certainly, just not a super-tech. Not even in my prime, and I was somewhat past my prime.

With yet another heavy sigh I turned from the computer, went over to the gun rack, and selected the deer-hunting rifle. I slung it and headed up the short ladder into the turret. The turret was originally a cooling turret of the sort seen on many barns, but now modified into a nice observation post. Originally meant to allow me to easily view my property, it now served as a sniper post. The only blind spot was the front and west side of the house, but a set of video monitors showed me the feed from the cameras for those areas. Everything seemed quiet. It appeared that the truce was holding despite my brief sojourn.

I lifted up the rifle and sighted through its scope to scan the surrounding area. The binoculars racked on the wall would have served the same purpose, of course. However, the rifle was better for a quick wide-area scan. It was also better for shooting at hostiles than the binoculars were.

Everything seemed calm at first glance as I took a look at my neighbours, looking at the signal lights on their roofs. Green for all was well, yellow for out of the house, and red for trouble. Everybody showed green, which was reassuring. Alas, not everyone took security as seriously as I did, so that was as good as I was going to get without physically visiting them. Which looked to be out of the question for the time being.

With a sigh, I toggled my own signal lights from yellow to green. Although I'm not the most sociable of men, I enjoyed meeting with my neighbours more often than every couple of months. The rural areas had more werewolf attacks than the cities, making regular visits dangerous. Things were better during the winter after the annual werewolf die-off. Life got back to a semblance of normal, and people tended to cram in a lot of social activities.

At other times of the year people tended to stay home, venturing out only for the periodic swap and barter meets. Travel for those events was done in a convoy escorted by OPP cruisers. There was a strict schedule, and people had learnt the hard way to travel only with those convoys.

Normally we'd use the phone lines to keep in touch and arrange the meets. The phone lines, along with the power, cable TV, and Internet connectivity, were buried and theoretically isolated from the elements. In practise, alas, water would sometimes seep in and short out sections for indeterminate lengths of time. That had been a problem from the day they were installed, corporate propaganda and denials to the contrary. The outages got worse as time went on. In fact, everything had been out of service for the past few weeks. Hopefully it would clear up sooner than later.

It'd be nice to get the next meet arranged, and see my neighbours again. Also nice to top up supplies of spices and perishables. That assumed, of course, that there were any to be had at any price. The staples were usually available, but for the past year or so anything imported seemed to be sucked up by the big cities, with decreasing amounts for the rest of us.

For now, though, I was still on my own and everything looked to be shipshape. I took one last look around through the gun's scope, and one last look at the video feeds. Everything looked clear. No need to worry, silly old man. I climbed down, racked the gun, walked down the stairs and prepared to exit the barn and enter the house.

Oh, wait—another task I had almost forgotten. I walked over to the sink and grabbed the watering can, then went around the interior watering all the various plants. The ubiquitous garlic and wolfsbane were there, of course, plus a few others meant just for brightening up the place. As the ritual demanded, I said a few words of encouragement to each of them as I gave them their water rations. I don't know if talking to them helped the plants, but it always seemed to ease my own mind a bit. Sort of like a mindfulness exercise.

Whatever. It was a small pleasure in a world increasingly devoid of pleasures, large or small. When the watering was over, I returned the watering can to the sink and filled it up for next time. The plants upstairs had been watered a day ago, so they would keep for a while.

After a brief look around to ensure that I'd not forgotten something, I was ready to head back to the house. I walked over to the gun cabinet and selected the shotgun to augment the revolver that I always wore. I did a check of the shotgun (oiled just last week, and always loaded) and racked a shell into the chamber. Walking over to the door, I peered through the spy-hole to confirm that it was safe to exit. Even with fancy electronics, the old eyeball was still the fail-safe system of choice. A very good habit to maintain.

I toggled the door switches to activate the solenoids that pulled back the security bolts. When those clicked into place, I opened the door and stepped a couple of paces outside before halting. I continued only after hearing the reassuring clack of bolts shooting back into their locked positions.

Walking without haste towards the house, I took the stairs leading to the porch one at a time. Used to be that I'd bound up, taking two or three steps at a time, but not anymore. My footfalls made a solid thunk on the stairs. I'd built that stairway out of two-inch heavy oak, replacing the rather flimsier pine steps that came with the house. Stepping onto the porch made a similar solid sound—I'd replaced a lot of boards in the porch, too.

Finally, I stopped at the door. I pulled the electronic key out from an inner pocket of my jacket and held it up. The door gave a satisfying clack as its bolts were pulled back by solenoids. I pushed it open, stepped in, then pushed it shut again. The bolts immediately slapped back into place, securing the door from anything short of explosives.

A quick glance at the indicator lights sunk into the moulding showed that no surprises had been detected inside the house while I'd been away. With a contented sigh I opened the inner door and stepped into the kitchen. I ejected the chambered shell from the shotgun and put it back into the magazine before racking the gun in its slot in the kitchen. Shrugging out of my jacket, I hung it between the door and shotgun so no intruder could easily get at the gun. As always, the holstered revolver stayed on my hip.

The savoury smell coming from the slow cooker made my mouth water. A quick wash-up and it would be time for supper. There was a time when I'd sit on the porch to eat and sip tea, watching the natural world unfold as I unwound from the day's work. Alas, those times were long gone.

Fucking werewolves. They had ruined everything.

CHAPTER THREE
Net Night

      I kept an eye on the clock as I ate my supper, and decided to forgo my usual glass of wine. It was Net Night, and I wanted to stay as sharp as possible. There were still a couple of hours before the Net started, so there was no need to rush. I'm a decent cook, and the stew had turned out well. The fresh bread added a nice contrast of taste and texture to the stew, and I washed it all down with some ice-cold water.

      With the meal finished, I gathered the dishes and pots and left them soaking in the sink. After boiling water and setting the tea to steep, I did the washing up and left the dishes to drip dry in the rack. Grabbing a tray, I put the pot of tea, a cup, and a few cookies on it before heading down to the basement. It was time to get ready.

      I carefully made my way down the stairs, holding the tray with a hand on either side. There was a time I'd simply have balanced it in the middle or held it with one hand, but a couple of messy spills had taught me that those days were behind me. However, I could turn on the lights with an elbow in passing, and I still got a kick out of that. Net Night always improved my mood, even if the discussions tended to be pretty damn somber these days.

      Reaching the bottom of the steps, I used my right knee to push open the partially open door at the bottom, and my right elbow to hit the light switch. Pausing for a moment, I balanced the tray with my left hand as I pressed it against my chest for support. I tapped at the flush-mounted switches with my right hand so the security system would recognize me as a friendly. With that done, the full lighting system engaged, and access to all the equipment allowed.

With the tray once more held by both hands I strolled to my desk, put the tray off to one side, pulled out the chair, and sat down. A quick scan of the monitors showed that my broadband connection was still down. This was not unexpected, just disappointing. It had been down for several weeks, and had been getting increasingly erratic for months. No big deal, it just meant that we'd have to use AX.25 over the ham bands again. Not the highest bandwidth, but worlds better than nothing.

My transceiver was already on, and I told the system to send a quick ID as it checked the status of the various digital repeaters on the 2-metre and 70-cm bands. The remaining ones these days were fairly dependable, though unforeseen outages were the new normal. The only one that showed as not responsive, I knew to be down for regular maintenance. After checking all their ping times, I decided to align my beam antennas towards the best digipeater in each band. It took a minute for the antennas to slew into position, time I used to drink some tea and nibble on a cookie. This was a new recipe, and I decided that it was a keeper, although the spices could use a bit of a tweak.

After the antennas finished slewing into position, I sat and watched the traffic headers on the signals I could see. There wasn't much traffic tonight, which was something to be thankful for, as it meant that we wouldn't have to share the limited bandwidth. Believe or not, there were still some idiots who insisted on trying to download movies over these limited bandwidths. As if a 1200-baud connection (2400-baud on a good day) was enough to download a movie. Idiots.

Alas, that limited amount of bandwidth meant that our conversations were limited to typing at each other. Like Twitter or IRC. I missed hearing their voices, though.

A glance at the clock showed that it was about twenty minutes until the net was scheduled to start. Most times people showed up early, but sometimes other commitments made that impossible. We made sure never to talk about substantive issues until the official start time. Politeness mattered these days—maybe more so than usual, come to think of it. I hoped that everyone would be able to make it. An unspoken, yet very real, fear was that one of our small number would fall prey to one of the dangers that lurked in increasing numbers.

Our little group—we simply called it "The Group"—had started before I even moved up here. Before the Change Plague got started. Just myself and a few friends in Toronto that I'd kept in contact with over the years, even after I moved to the hinterlands northwest of Orangeville. People drifted in and out of The Group, but eventually a core group of eight formed.

As times got stranger and harder, I enlarged my vegetable gardens and kept them supplied with some fresh vegetables on my periodic trips to Toronto. I hadn't been able to get down to see them since last fall, and I depended on these Net Nights to keep in contact.

City or rural, food was a big issue these past couple of years. With the werewolves gaining ground in the rural areas, the stores had turned to foreign suppliers. When those shipments started to dry up, the stores once again turned to local farmers. The solution to the werewolf attacks on small trucks was to either have larger trucks (not always possible on back roads) or convoys of trucks with a police escort. The dairy farmers got visited once or twice a week throughout the year. Produce farmers would get visits only during the harvest season. So most farmers went back to mixed farming, with some meat production of some sort in the mix. Chickens and pigs were popular here in the East, with cattle more so in the West.

Of course, the big food companies claimed that convoys increased costs (although independent studies showed that it was cheaper and more efficient), and that claim allowed them to pay farmers less and charge consumers more. Anyway, if travel was required farmers would take advantage of these convoys and join in with them. In my case, I was off on a side-road never used for any of the big convoys. The only convoys I ever saw were the ones put together for the infrequent barter and swap meets. No telling when the next one would be. Until then, I was safe enough on my farm.

Fucking werewolves.

A series of musical notes announcing the start of the Net shook me out of my reverie. Damn—no-one had come on early. That did not bode well, and my unease blossomed into outright fear when only five of The Group—Stan Filson, Dixon Wells, Lee Neilan, and Grant Calthorpe, and myself. As usual, Stan was the designated moderator, so we all waited for him to start us off.

StanF : Hi everyone. Before you get too concerned, Jack and Clio are here with me. Their rig is acting up, so they hoofed it over to my place. Anyone else doubling up?

LeeN : Hi, guys. Gail is here with me. Power is out at her place and she wanted to save the batteries for emergencies.

DixonW : Any chance of going voice tonight?

StanF : Nope. All the voice repeaters are tied up by other people.

StanF : OK, Group, we should get on with it.

StanF : First of all, let's deal with necessities. Gail, are you ok where you are or do you need to move somewhere safer?

We always started our meetings with a discussion of the necessities of life. We discussed Gail's situation for a while, and it began to sound like her living arrangements were getting somewhat iffy. Lee offered to take her in. This was awfully nice of Lee, given that she had a small one-bedroom apartment.

The truth was, though, that times were getting rough and the outlook for the future wasn't at all rosy. Lee was in one of the older, smaller apartment buildings and those seemed to be holding up better than the newer high-rises for some reason. Stan had a small house in an older neighbourhood, and was fairly safe. I suspected that Jack and Clio would be moving out of their apartment into his place in the not-too-distant future.

Some of us were amateur gardeners, and we used to swap plants and veggies. As things started to break down, that began to take on a more urgent flavour. Now it boiled down to helping each other stay safe in an increasingly unsafe world. With food in short supply—and periodic de facto rationing going on in the cities—my own periodic trips to Toronto usually included a goodly supply of fresh veggies and sometimes meat. Between the snow, lack of road plowing maintenance, and late start to the growing season, I'd not been able to help my friends for far too long. Time for me to chime in.

FelixK : I've got some early potatoes and carrots and onions that are nearly ready for harvest. My new greenhouse is completed, but I had problems getting the soil and crops stabilized, but things look OK now. That'll give us some extra year-round food. The trick is going to be getting to you. I took a short trip out today, but had to cut it short on account of the w/wolves. They're acting real strange these days. More feral. More hunting-mode. Sitting in groups and singles alongside the road. I seem bottled up here—nothing in or out. Haven't talked with any neighbours in several months, but signal lights show all is OK. What's it like near you?

Now we were getting to the meat of the discussion. I'd always figured that my farm would be a fail-safe bolt-hole for the group. However, there were a couple problems with that. First of all, they had to somehow get here, and that was starting to look a lot more difficult than anyone expected. Secondly, my friends were city folk to the core. That is, they loved living in Toronto and simply couldn't conceive of a situation dire enough to force them to leave. They were each of them brilliant and insightful, but, damn, could they ever be stubborn.

    StanF : My own observations are that the
w/wolves are only a problem at night, and only in
certain areas like the ravines. Even so, there are
a lot fewer sightings and attacks than this time
last year. Jack wants me to add that his contacts
have confirmed that the wolves have taken over the
ravine system. The authorities are going to force
anyone left in houses near there to move out.

    LeeN : They seem to have left the subway
tunnels, so the trains are running mostly on time
these days.

    DixonW : The police claim to have forced them
out of the downtown core.

What followed were a lot of rude comments. We'd all
heard that one before, and it was always temporary. Last year
had been especially brutal. With luck, this year's trend of few
attacks would continue.

    GrantC : Anyone got any hard info on head
counts of the w/wolves?

    StanF : Jack says his contacts think that the
spring numbers are lower than normal. That, plus
the w/wolves concentrating in the ravines,
accounts for the success that the police are
claiming credit for.

This was important information. Normally, early
spring was when their numbers slowly began re-appearing.
People could move around with some degree of safety until
later in the year.

    FelixK : That's good news, but I'm seeing
more than normal out here in the boonies. Can't
confirm with my neighbours because phones are still
down. Tried to drive out to them today, but the
wolves were out in numbers and acting more

aggressive. Had to turn back.

        LeeN : Sorry to hear that, but smart move on
your part. Too many Fearless Fools out there.

She was right about discretion being the better part of
valour. Every year, there were a lot of deaths of people who
figured that the werewolves were just dumb beasts who
couldn't stand up to a "real man" (and the idiots were always
male). So many, in fact, that there was now a nickname for
their type of idiocy.

        DixonW : Hey, Felix, did you hear about the
results of the latest trials in the US?

        FelixK : No. Internet has been down for
weeks.

        DixonW : The killers got off. The juries
bought the self-defence crap. Again.

Well, that was interesting. The Change Plague hit
Canada hard, and only a few regions in the US had many
problems with it at all. For whatever reason, the worst of the
Change Plague hit up here. And yet the worst panic seemed to
hit regions in the US that had the fewest problems. In fact, the
main reason for problems there was due to panics and
overreactions to the few cases they did have. The worst of it
were the werewolf hunts—gangs of crazies with weapons that
went on what were in effect "wild hunts". Anyone with too
much hair, or the wrong coloured skin, was chased down and
killed. The victims were only rarely werewolves. Hell, they'd
even shot up truckers. As if werewolves could drive, much less
use tools of any sort.
        Charges of assault or murder were sometimes laid, yet
to date no-one had ever been convicted. It was a toxic
combination of "stand your ground" laws, the unholy marriage
of the NRA with the evangelical doomsday cults, and
say-anything-to-get-elected politics. We spent a few minutes

worrying about the effect this might have on the crazies up here. To date, nothing like that had happened up here—although there were some ugly rumours coming out of Alberta. Nothing official, but the rumours wouldn't go away.

After we ran that topic into the ground, Stan tried to steer the conversation into a new track. Alas, his words quickly dissolved into garbled fragments. Damn. It was either equipment failure in the repeater or some asshole jamming us.

```
StanF : OK, better wrap it up. Use email to
keep in touch. 73.
```

As we started typing out our goodbyes, the data stream degenerated into gibberish. Damn jammers. Probably wanted to hijack the repeater to download a movie. Idiots. Well, at least we got to touch base and exchange a little information. Things didn't seem to be too dire for my friends, so there was no need for any panic-driven action. We had a few months before things got serious enough to worry about.

That got me thinking about my neighbours, and my aborted attempt to visit them. Had I turned back too easily? My guilt gnawed at me, despite my analytical mind stomping on that. Werewolf numbers in my area had been up way more than normal, and the damn things acted more feral. In recent years too many people around here had gotten injured or killed by underestimating them.

I heaved a long, heartfelt sigh, reached for my mug, and drained the tea. I'd put the uneaten cookies back into their container in the kitchen. Glancing at the computer I could see that the repeaters and digipeaters were all tied up, so there'd be no more Net Night.

A quick glance at the security system showed that it was cool enough for the infrared cameras to work properly, allowing me to do a check of the area with those. The werewolves were staying on the far side of the road, although it seemed to me that they were moving around more than usual and that there were more of them.

Damn. It was going to be a long spring and longer

summer.

I decided to call it a night, and took the tray back up to the kitchen, taking care the turn out the lights and reset the security system as I left the basement. A new day, and its attendant problems, would be arriving all too soon.

CHAPTER FOUR
Dancing With Data

The next morning brought to me a world where the phone and data lines were still dead, all the voice and data repeaters were locked up or dead, solar storms or something were screwing up radio and satellite reception, and the werewolves were prowling around just outside my property line. Left entirely to my own isolated little world, I focused on the dull, dirty chores that had been put off.

I expanded the garden beds around the greenhouse, planted garlic and wolfsbane in the newly-dug garden beds (and made a note to start propagating more, as I was now out of new stock), built up and stirred the compost piles, that sort of thing. It was a warmish early-spring day, and it felt wonderful to be outside. I ended the day feeling comfortably worn out and at peace with the world. If it weren't for the damn werewolves prowling around it would have been a fine way to spend one's life.

With the physical side of survival taken care of for the next week or two, I decided to work out some more contingency plans. The little bit of news I'd managed to get during the last Net Night had been nagging away at me as I worked.

That didn't bother me. I'd learnt long ago to let a puzzle sit in the back of my head until my mind had gnawed on it sufficiently. The key thing nagging me, aside from the general worry for the safety of my friends, was the increased numbers of the wolves so early in the year. The official numbers didn't seem to match with what I was seeing.

The other strange thing was that the wolves seemed to be concentrating in certain areas. In the past, they tended to be more or less spread out and flowed through areas in a few waves each season. That could just be observer bias, yet how else to explain their large numbers around my area and lesser numbers in Toronto? It was all very strange. Someone in The Group would distribute newer data when they could get their hands on it, but maybe I should take another look at what I already had to see if there was a pattern I'd missed.

That night I went to bed early, glad for weariness born of physical work and a technical problem to worry over. Much easier on my nerves than worrying about neighbours and friends.

The next morning I put a small roast in the slow cooker and set it up to work its culinary magic while I went to the basement to go dancing with the data. Sure, all sorts of people had already pushed and prodded and munged the same data and found nothing. Or, rather, sometimes found illusionary correlations and false positives. The newsgroups were full of wild speculations fuelled by those illusions. On the other hand, I knew what I was doing.

OK, I was only a retired data twiddler and not up on all the fanciest algorithmic funkiness, but I knew how to slice and dice data better than most folks who claimed to be experts. Had proved it more than once by rubbing the noses of those so-called experts in their mistaken analysis. Which far too often got me passed over for promotions and raise. It turned out that being a self-important asshole with fancy degrees and the right contacts was more important than technical competence.

Still, despite being increasingly frozen out of the business loop I would sometimes be quietly brought in to help on delicate tasks that needed someone with a nose for patterns—a data dancer. That sort of talent, and a reputation for being able to keep my mouth shut when asked, had gotten me in contact with a varied and interesting collection of people over the years. This was how I had met several members of The Group, in fact.

In any event, in the absence of anything urgent clamouring

for attention, I needed a problem to work on. My feelings of helplessness, stemming from being unable to help my friends or neighbours, were spinning around and around inside my head. Not the best mental state to be in. And maybe I could figure out why the werewolves were so thick on the ground, so early in the year.

I took a quick glance at the networking links and confirmed that they were all still down. A check of the security system showed that everything was clear, although I decided to make the system a bit more sensitive to possible problems. That would increase the false positives, but I tended to get overly focused when working and wouldn't be paying attention to security. Time to let the automatics do that for me.

The first task was to make some coffee. While it was brewing, I warmed up the shortwave receiver to see if the ether gods would smile upon me this day. I'm a news junkie and hadn't been able to get a fix for a few days. Local radio stations, when I could receive them, were usually devoid of hard news. Worse, they were all located in the cities and increasingly parochial in their viewpoint, ignoring anything beyond city limits.

I'm not sure why the local stations were getting so hard to receive, although reducing their power to save money was certainly part of it. With the rarity of newspapers in rural areas, radio and television filled that void. The only station that always came in reliably was the CBC. Alas, they were now forbidden by law from competing against commercial interests and only allowed to broadcast for a couple of hours twice a week. Those were the only decent news shows available, too. Hence my checking of the shortwave bands for international stations. In these days of the Internet, however, these were increasingly rare.

Still, many of the smaller countries found it a cost-effective way to make their voices heard. No matter how hard the solar winds blew, normally I could pick up something for a little bit. Ah, and there it was—scratchy and fading in and out, but I could pick it out well enough. Some sort of non-English singing, which was interesting. After a few minutes of that, a male voice came on and yakked for a handful of seconds as the signal faded away into the background static.

With a disappointed sigh, I turned off the radio and started up some soft classical music from my collection. It was time to get to work. I pulled out the box with the printouts of graphs from previous analysis attempts, and arranged them on the floor in a matrix. My initial setup sorted them chronologically from oldest to newest, left to right. From there I sorted the data for each year with common data in the same row. That way I could spot gaps for any specific type of data in any given year. I also left a gap between each year, so that I could easily walk around the sheets without disturbing them too much.

I would have preferred to tack them up off the ground, but I didn't have enough bare wall space. I liked to spread it all out like this, to make it easier to see everything at a glance or to quickly zoom in on specific things. That couldn't be done on a computer monitor, or at least not as well.

Speaking of which, I sat down and brought up my usual suite of analysis programs and language-specific IDE's, and opened up file folders with the raw data. That would let me quickly do any specific data twiddling if I needed to do that. All that remained to do was to pour myself a cup of coffee and do a quick scan of the printouts on the floor to familiarize myself with the overview of it.

With the preliminaries completed, I sat down to review my notes from the previous analysis attempts. Yes, of course I had notes. It was one of things that separated the no-talent hacks from the professionals.

It took a half hour, and two cups of coffee, before I felt properly back up to speed. I got up, stretched, and slowly walked amongst the graphs, with my hands clasped behind my head. Nothing new popped out at me. And none of it made sense. Oh, sure, it was easy enough to make pretty charts and calculate residuals and standard deviations and all that fancy stuff. It's just that none of it explained anything useful. None of it explained what the hell was happening, how it happened, or what we could expect in the short- or long-term future.

A quick glance at the security systems showed me that

nothing had changed. Same old yard and fields, same old werewolves prowling around the edges and staying on their side of the fences.

Fucking werewolves.

It all began with amateur biologists—biohackers—teaming up with body modders and crank sociologists. Taking gene therapy technologies and tweaking them to suit the desires of fools. Using gene therapies originally designed to help people, then splicing DNA from wild animals into them. What could possibly go wrong with that?

Maybe it was all those computer games and movies about magic that got people used to the idea of quaffing magical potions to change into some animal or other. Or maybe it was the dumbfuck psychobabble "experts" proclaiming that we should get in touch with our inner spirit animal. Or maybe it was the ecofools who wanted everyone to get more in touch with Nature.

There's never been a shortage of idiots.

Then along came a technology that would allow them indulge in their idiocy. Some wanted to be able to think like a favourite animal, and others wanted to gain their physical attributes. The Internet was filled with rapturous postings promising a Golden Future.

In the beginning, some years ago, the first attempts at inducing Changes into people failed. How could they not? No-one knew what the hell they were doing. All too quickly, someone figured how to puree the appropriate parts of an animal's brain, extract the RNA, and map that to the DNA sequences. That began a few successes at altering human behaviour to be more like a specific animal's. As strange as it got, it was limited to a small group of idiots in just a few places. Mainly California, funnily enough.

Ever seen a human crawling on the ground and flicking their tongue like a lizard? Looked real funny until it turned out that the person wasn't joking, and the human part seemed to be lost. The attempts by the body modders produced some ugly clumps of fur, scales, and feathers. Again, limited to isolated groups of idiots.

When the media made a big deal out of all this, all the experts made assurances that because of the biological techniques used any of these so-called treatments would have to be injected. Which meant that the only threat was to whomever agreed to the injections. It could absolutely never be changed into a communicable disease.

Then it happened.

I tried to think of an appropriate curse, but profanity failed me.

No-one knew how, or if they did they weren't telling. The first communicable Change Plagues weren't terribly contagious, and results could be almost comical. For example, people would catch a cold then start to act like a chipmunk. There were all sorts of small outbreaks, of all sorts of very specific Changes. Some affected only behaviour, some modified body features, but it was always one specific type of animal.

That was the first summer outbreak. With the coming of winter all the Change diseases just stopped, and all the Affected died. Little serious harm had been done, causalities were limited to a handful of people, and everyone breathed a sigh of relief.

When springtime came, the Change diseases came back. Stronger, more virulent, and with a combination of behaviour and physical changes. That's when people began calling it the Change Plague.

Anyway, that's what my graphs showed—the ebb and flow of the Change Plague with the seasons. The increase in virulence each year. The increase in the amount of change that each new strain produced in people. The die-off of the Changed every winter. Why did they die? One theory was that they were feral animals locked inside a body that was just plain wrong for their survival. A human with the instincts and behaviour of, say, a chipmunk wouldn't be able to survive as one.

That's when some of the more vicious Changed started to attack the unaffected. It was pretty horrific the first few times—very newsworthy. It stayed that way for a couple of years, and people adapted to the cycle of it. Treated it as just another threat to be avoided in the non-winter months. In any event, there weren't all that many attacks, nasty though they were.

All that changed when the Change Plague altered and produced only predator types. The non-predator Changed simply stopped appearing. That's when the media took to calling the Changed "werewolves". It was a one-way change, unlike in the movies or books, but it made a great sound bite and sounded really catchy. The increased hairiness and enhanced healing helped to cement the meme.

Hard to know what the Changed thought of all this, as research into helping them decreased as their numbers and ferocity increased. They died back each winter, and early spring was always a hopeful time when people could go about their lives without fear of being attacked. My graphs were based on the official numbers, and showed the numbers of the Changed to be reaching a maximum before levelling off each year, with no more increases above a certain level. It was being contained—or so the data seemed to be saying.

The problem with that view was that each year the social fabric got more and more frayed. The physical infrastructure that bound together our society became less and less reliable. Worse, the official numbers were based on sightings in and near the cities. Given what I'd been seeing the past year, I was beginning to conclude that the official numbers were not just inadequate, but horribly wrong. Things were a lot worse than the numbers indicated, and about to get a whole lot worse damn quickly.

That was just a hunch, though, and I've had hunches go wrong often enough that I'd learnt the importance of putting a lot of trust in data and my ability to analyze it. That only works when one has faith in the data, and I was losing faith in my data. My hands clenched and gripped my head as I groaned in frustration.

A soft musical trilling interrupted my cogitations. Grateful for any interruption, I sprang to console desk. The breeze created by my passage scattered the papers behind me. I wasn't worried by the alert, as it wasn't a security alarm. A quick scan of the various monitors showed that a blinking icon on the environmental sensor suite—my magnetometer was indicating a large and persistent drop in the solar activity, which indicated that the current solar storm was over. About damn time, too, considering that this was supposed to be a "quiet sun" interval.

Another soft warble came from the communications monitor as it announced that satellite communications was beginning to re-establish itself. Welcome news, as it meant access to news channels and just possibly a usable data link. Internet access via satellite was a tedious business, with narrow uplink bandwidth and modest downlink bandwidth. Despite those limitations, it could be a real lifeline when the landline links were down. Unfortunately, it could take a while before satellite comms got back up to speed after a solar storm—maybe minutes, maybe hours.

There was only one sensible thing to do. I went upstairs to the kitchen and made some bread. I even added some of my diminishing supply of raisins, after soaking them in some rum to plump them up. For flavour, you understand. Leaving the dough to rise, I decided to do a quick security prowl through the house before going back downstairs.

I liked to do these checks by the numbers. The shotgun by the kitchen door was secure and ready. The doors to the outside, front and back, were secure. I slid my revolver out of its holster at my hip, and entered the greenhouse.

Of necessity, the greenhouse was the least secure area of the house what with all the glass. Despite that, it was probably going to become terribly important as a year-round means of supplying food. The security indicators all showed green or else I wouldn't have entered it at all. However, I was trying to maintain the habit of care when entering it.

It was a decent-sized greenhouse, too, measuring four by eight metres. Large enough that there was a centre isle in addition to the plants along the sides, which were sufficient to obscure the view within.

As I walked through the area, I performed through the "security dance" I had developed. It was sort of like a martial arts kata, with a structured approach that forced me to look everywhere in the greenhouse while maintaining my balance and focus. Sometimes I would do the exercise with a gun of some sort, and sometimes with an edged weapon, but the basics were always the same. My steps were more like glides, and I took care to maintain a controlled centre of gravity as I stepped and spun my way up and down the aisles, squatting to peer under the tables, and always in constant motion.

It wasn't that I was a martial arts guru—even a white belt student would have laughed at my efforts. Still, it was the best procedure I could think of, and excellent exercise. With the security sweep completed I repeated the walk-through, this time taking care to look at the plants themselves. All the while, the revolver stayed in my hands.

Everything looked healthy—the carrots and onions seemed to be coming along nicely, and the potatoes were beginning to poke up enough that it would soon be time to add another layer of soil on top of them. I liked growing potatoes. One seed potato can grow dozens more so long as you keep dumping soil on top of it as it grows in a container.

There were a couple of containers made of old tires. I simply plopped another tire on the top and added soil. Most of my potato containers were made of thick wood, each a metre square by fifteen centimetres deep. I just needed to add another module and some more soil every so often. Container gardening at its best.

There were also some strawberries growing in tubular baskets that I hung from the ceiling. Scattered about were the usual plantings of garlic and wolfsbane. This was where I started the propagations for them, and they also served as a last-ditch defence.

After examining the plants, I did a quick check of the watering and ventilation systems. As expected, the various sensors had told the truth about their status. It always paid to verify what the sensors told you, just in case the sensor itself or its communication link had gone bad.

Realizing that time was a-wasting, I took one last contented look around and exited the greenhouse. Holstering the revolver, I closed and secured the door before going to the kitchen. After washing my hands, I punched down the bread dough and left it to do the second rise. A large glass of water and bio-break later, I headed back to the basement to get back to work.

I walked into the basement, and what to my wondering eyes did appear but a screen full of email headers indicating the satellite link was up and had access to the Internet. Oh, frabjous day. Callooh, callay. Also hot damn.

I forced myself to get a fresh cup of coffee before sitting down to read the email. Was pleased to note that my hands were only shaking a little bit. Walking carefully to the chair to avoid spilling any coffee, I sat down with a contented sigh to examine the bounty provided for me. After a quick glance I started to chuckle, which quickly turned into outright laughter.

The world was in danger of coming to an end, and yet Nigerian princes were still pleased to inform me that I was eligible to claim vast sums of money if only I would send them my personal details. I chuckled as I deleted them. There were a few more spam messages that I was able to delete unread—I had no need for sex pills or hookups with hot singles in my area.

My faith in humanity thus restored, I made a more careful scan of the emails. There were a couple from my bank, which I'd look at later, as there was nothing in the subject line that indicated urgency. I paused over a couple of emails from distant relatives and former colleagues. Was tempted to delete those unread. With a sigh, I moved them to the "to be read later" file.

I'd been starting to hear from a few people that I'd not heard from in years. Had minimal contact with them even at the best of times. Now, each one was reaching out to renew our previous "deep friendship" or to "heal old wounds", in these trying times. Uh-huh. And to suck up to a possible provider of a safe haven in the event things went truly bad. They were quite blatant about it, and I was sorely tempted to tell them what to do with themselves. Still, so long as they stayed civil, I would as well. Not to encourage them—oh, hell, no. It was just that I had always found it difficult to be hard-nosed about pushing people away. Never having had too many people in my life at the best of times, I never got much practise at it. However, I did have it on good authority that I did have a talent for pissing people off in all sorts of ways.

With the cruft sorted out, I finally bent to looking at the gold that remained. And gold it was—messages from friends in The Group, some with attachments. Those were typically pictures, which was of increasing importance given the diminished ability to meet in person. Heck, even people living in the same city had to be careful when meeting up these days. The only safe times were during business hours, and even then only in the core areas. With survival taking precedence, physical meet-ups between scattered friends was becoming rarer.

The first email had some welcome news. Gail was moving in with Lee, as there was damage to the electrical transformer in Gail's apartment building that would take anywhere from a couple of weeks to a couple of months to fix. Both ladies worked at the Royal Ontario Museum, so that also allowed them to get to and from work together. Gail would be moving her stuff over the next few days, or sooner if they could arrange for movers. The attached picture showed them both smiling over a glass of wine as they toasted the move. Good people—smart and tough, the both of them.

Stan sent a general newsletter email to make sure that everyone was up to speed on the latest news. On his own home front, Jack and Clio were seriously considering moving in with him. As I recalled, his house was more defensible than an apartment, and had a nice back yard that got enough sun for proper gardening. He had planted a lot of hedge roses, garlic, and wolfsbane around the borders, and had convinced his adjoining neighbours to do the same. There were even TTC bus and streetcar routes close by. His house was on the small side, so things might get cozy. I suspected that none of them would mind that in the least. Ah, youth.

The last email was from Dixon, and came with an attachment. He meant well and was plenty intelligent, but lacked smarts. I was quite sure that only his exposure to The Group kept him from haring off with some of his hacker buddies into doing truly stupid stunts. These days he focused his excessive energies into rooting out tidbits of information and generally trying to be helpful.

Sometimes he came up with the info more interesting than useful. Sometimes, though, his stuff was pure gold, and came from an eclectic range of contacts. He really, really needed to get laid and settle down. As it was, he seemed content with his lifestyle of graphic novels, books, and computers. His friend, Grant, helped to keep Dixon in line despite being of the nerd clan as well. All in all, good lads.

So it was with a soft sigh that I opened up his latest attachment. As expected, it was compressed with a password and I started going through our standard list of them. Dix had devised a system for encryption, with different passwords reserved for different levels of importance, and was quite strict about sticking to that. He was also careful—even paranoid—about ensuring that whatever he sent was safe to open, so I had no compunctions about looking at anything that came from him.

I was going through the list of passwords, and escalating up the levels of importance with no luck so far. I was developing a frown, which got seriously deep when I reached the point of having only two passwords left. The next one was Top Level Stuff, and the last was All-Hell-Breaking-Loose. It turned out to be the latter.

At this point I sat back with an unhappy grunt. Dix had never sent anything with that level before. Curiosity soon won, and I saved the file to my local system before opening it. It was a single, large database that looked to be an enumeration of sightings, infection rates, that sort of thing. Just like the data I already had, except this was far more extensive. For one thing, it had geographic codes attached to the sightings, and those seemed to be for the entire country. Oh, my. That *was* new, as the only data we had been able to get to date applied only to Toronto and the GTA.

Where the hell had this come from? It was no use asking where Dix had got it from—he'd only shrug nonchalantly as if it were no big thing and not answer. Taking another look, I saw that there was also a small text file that I'd overlooked. With a snort of disgust at my foolish oversight, I took a look at it .

Well, knock me down and paint me pink: if the text file was kosher, this was a top secret database from the Department of Defence. In the olden days—that is, pre-Plague—I would have been worried. Now, though, I was not overly surprised. The normal social structures were becoming seriously frayed, with the result that personal connections were becoming more and more important. Loyalties shifted to keeping family and friends safe. Whatever his faults, Dixon was intensely loyal to his friends. The Group tended to reciprocate, and I wasn't surprised that his other friends did as well.

The first cut at the analysis went pretty quickly, as I could use the programs that I had used on the original data. A few minor tweaks to deal with the slightly different format were all it took before I could start the analysis running. The first thing to do would be to simply load it in preparation for analysis, then check for problems. Given the size of the database this would easily take fifteen minutes, if not longer.

I used the time to work on a way to make use of the geographic data. The analysis currently running would give me an overall picture for Canada as a whole, and that would be interesting to compare to the Toronto data. My first thought was to break things down by province, rather than drill down to individual cities. That would give a broad regional overview. It could also be handled by my existing program, with a few small mods. Those changes were quickly implemented, and I set that analysis to running.

Waiting for the analysis to finish gave me time to ponder on ways to get a finer-grained geographic analysis. The formally correct way would be to create a hexagonal grid overlaying the country and do the analysis for each element in the grid. That would take a long time to run, and would probably be worthwhile to do at some point. Then it hit me—filter the data by city. Using cities and towns above a certain size would give a few roughly scattered cells in each province. Good enough for a first look.

When the first analysis finished, I printed out the graphs it had produced. While waiting for those, I wrote the code for the coarse grid approach, and set it running. With a sigh, I leaned back in the chair. The resultant cramp in my back was a forcible reminder of how stiff I could get when sitting too long in one position. Like when getting absorbed by a problem.

Time to get up and move about for a bit.

I stood up, not bothering to stifle the groans drowned out by the popping sounds made by stiff joints. I hobbled around for a minute to unkink my aged body. It was probably past time to go back upstairs to set the bread to baking. Climbing up the stairs felt like a major effort, but got easier with each step. By the time I got to the top I was only feeling ten years older than I actually was.

After checking that the bread had risen sufficiently, I set the oven to start heating up while I took a brief bio-break and checked the security system. It was mid-afternoon by this time, and the ranks of the watching werewolves had thinned out. Probably off hunting. The one benefit of having them around was that they kept the local rabbit and small rodent population in check. The area had never been so vermin-free. On the negative side, alas, was the loss of any pets that wandered too far from home.

When the oven got up to temperature I popped the bread in and set the timer on the stove. I also set the timer on my cell phone, and put that back into its belt holster. Fresh-baked bread was too important to take chances with.

With that vital chore completed, I headed back downstairs to check on the analysis runs. Upon entering the basement, the first thing I did was to collect the graphs sitting in the output trays of the printers. I wasn't worried about using up paper and toner, as I'd stocked up on such things a few years back and had kept up the stocking levels whenever possible. The other two analysis runs were still ongoing, giving me time to grab some coffee and take a look at the graphs.

To fuel the upcoming effort, I took a few careful sips of the hot coffee. Once fortified, I began putting the newly-calculated graphs for the country as a whole on top of their equivalent graphs for Toronto. My brow furrowed at the noticeable differences after the first year. By the time I'd laid the graphs for all years, I was far beyond the frowning stage. Every year showed a greater discrepancy between the two sets of graphs, and where Toronto's appeared to level off, the national data kept getting worse.

It looked like my hunch from this morning might be right.

Once the province-by-province analysis finished, I took a look at the graphs on the monitor, rather than printing them out. There was little good news there. Although the usual winter die-off showed up, there was no levelling off of rates of infestation. The more I looked at it, the more the hunch-emitting part of my mind started to tingle. I was missing something important.

Suddenly I realized what had been bothering me. The rates of infections were going up in spite of total die-offs of the infected each winter. In fact, it was only this last winter that didn't have significant die-offs. This was the case both nationally and for each province. Something was not right. I dimly remembered researching disease infection curves some time ago.

After scanning the brief notes I had left on the computer, I started rooting through my notebooks for handwritten notes. It turned out to be almost three years ago that I'd looked into this. There it was: equations for rates of infection, disease spreads, and suchlike. I'd not gotten much further into it, as I had been going into serious survival mode at the time. The official data had indicated a levelling off, the winter's die-off had made everyone complacent, and I had simply forgotten about it until now. Something about those curves bothered my subconscious, and quite a lot.

Going back to the computer I decided to set up another type of analysis, one which looked at the data from the viewpoint of disease spread. Plagues normally come and go. The Ebola outbreaks, for example, came, stopped for years, re-occurred, went dormant again for years, and finally stopped reappearing. Same thing with the Black Death, way back in Medieval Europe. A couple waves of death that killed off thirty to fifty percent of the population. After that it was gone, with only the rare case popping up every so often. There was a lot of research on tracking and predicting outbreaks, and somehow I'd never applied that to the Change Plague. It was past time that I did so.

I kept at it for several hours, ignoring the alerts that signalled that the bread was ready, and only taking a break to take the blackened husk of bread out of the oven and turning on the fans to remove the smoke. I hurried back downstairs to continue working.

The problem consumed my attention until, several hours later, my analysis was complete. I ran the analysis using both my old data and the most recent data sent by Dix. The old data showed infection curves similar to something like a cold or flu—hanging around for a while, then eventually levelling off just prior to vanishing forever. Textbook curve, in fact.

The new data, the probably classified data, showed a different story. The Change Plague did, in fact, appear to go dormant each winter. However, the curves weren't for a single disease that went dormant and re-appeared. The curves quite clearly showed that every year's outbreak spread in a different way, getting steadily more effective each year. A check of my notes showed that this was different from the usual seasonal flu and cold viruses. This was like a brand new virus each year, rather than one virus that mutated slightly from one year to the next. This was different from any viral outbreak on record.

That would imply—hell, it damn near proved—that someone was re-establishing a new and improved version of the Change Plague every year. The geographic analysis showed that it was occurring across the country at roughly the same time—within days, in fact. That wasn't how diseases normally spread.

I twiddled with the database to see if I could see any patterns in the spread—something about the timescale bothered me. Maybe that would give a clue about how it was being spread. That required just a few tweaks to my program, and less than an hour later I had my results. The numbers refused to talk to me like they normally did. I stubbornly attributed that to exhaustion rather than age. To help figure out what was going on I kludged up something that would show the spread over time, overlaid on a map. Given the coarseness of the time-scale,

I set the increments to twice a day.

I advanced the image from one time period to the next by tapping a key. Tap, pause, tap, pause, and so on until it completed and had started to loop back to the beginning. It didn't make any sense, yet if the data was valid, this was as close an approximation to reality as I was going to get. The conclusions seemed inescapable.

Someone was using the Change Plague on an ongoing basis to destroy the world.

They seemed to be getting better at it.

Each new Change Plague started in Toronto, and radiated more or less uniformly outwards at an unnatural speed.

CHAPTER FIVE
A Trail of Breadcrumbs

As unnerving as the results of my analysis were, I was too numb to feel much—a sure sign that my brain was fried and that it was time for bed. I carefully saved and backed up all my work, and the fact that it took longer than it should have was a sure sign of brain-melt. When that task was completed I stumbled upstairs and crawled into bed.

Annoyingly, my mind was still buzzing, making sleep impossible. Argh—stupid brain. Exhausted as I was, it wanted to keep going. Fine. I began thinking about all the chores I needed to do, and was soon fast asleep. Sometimes escapism was a useful tool.

I woke up just before dawn, feeling quite a bit better. Bouncing out of bed, I checked the nearby security readouts to confirm that everything was fine, then had a shower and changed. Once that was completed, I did another check of the security readouts before heading downstairs for breakfast.

What remained of the old bread was getting somewhat hard by this time, so I settled for some boiled oats. While it was cooking I decided that it was time to take another stab at making some fresh bread. It didn't take long to mix everything and set it aside for the first rising.

When my breakfast was ready, I sat down and planned out my day as I ate. There were always chores of one sort or another to do, of course. However, as there was nothing urgent, I decided to go back to data dancing. The fact that it was more fun than any of the other chores had absolutely no bearing on my decision. None at all. The fact that it was terribly important was also a factor.

As punishment for my self-indulgence, I decided to forgo coffee and drink tea instead. To make up for being so mean to myself I grabbed a few cookies to take downstairs along with the tea. It was important to be tough, but fair.

Sitting down at my computer, I did a quick review of the analysis I had done the previous night. Early morning. Whatever.

The single biggest gap in my analysis, it seemed to me, was the crudeness of the geographic analysis. My first cut had looked only at Canadian data, so my distribution analysis might be just a teeny bit skewed. The first thing I did was check to see if there was any data for outside of Canada. Turns out that there was information for the rest of North America in a different section of the database. Damn, where had Dixon gotten this stuff?

I repeated my analysis with the new data. To make profitable use of the waiting time I made another cup of tea, munched on a cookie, and checked the security systems. Doing the systems check took less than a minute, despite trying to draw it out. That left me with time to think. Too many questions, and not enough answers.

Or ... maybe not.

Was I asking the right questions? That was an important point to ponder, and a key part of successful analysis. Alrighty then, what sorts of questions was I not asking? I had a bunch of data and lots of pretty graphs as a result of crunching the numbers for the spread of the Change Plague. Hmm, given the rapid geographic spread why was the actual number of the infected so low? Yeah, that was one of the questions I hadn't thought to ask until now, that's for sure.

The number of victims of the Change Plague was actually surprisingly small, as a fraction of the population. In fact, the Plague virus itself was quite fragile and could be destroyed by UV lights and relatively mild disinfectants. There were no reported cases of people becoming infected by the corpses of the Changed, or even after being bitten by them.

How it actually got transmitted, and who was vulnerable to it, had been a big mystery for the first couple years of its existence. Without any answers forthcoming, though, people came to simply accept that it happened, coming back each spring like clockwork. The gradual breakdown of society seemed to focus people's concerns on the immediate necessities of life. That included medical research.

Thinking about infection got me thinking about the yearly die-off. What was it that they were dying of, exactly? Sure, living rough in the wilds was dangerous and hard. That was enough to account for the first couple of year's worth of Changed. However, with the appearance of the werewolf type came an enhanced healing. Each year's lot of Changed was tougher and better at healing than the last. So why was there an annual die-off every winter?

Which brought up yet another unasked question—the first of the Change Plagues started in California, so why was Toronto now a centre for it? Hmm, best to hold off on that one until the results of the latest analysis was in. I needed to confirm that the centre had, indeed, shifted.

Speaking of California, that's how the acceptance of it started, come to think of it. The fact that someone was idiotic enough to experiment on themselves was a cause for scorn. The early results were treated as jokes—until it was realized that the victims weren't going to recover. But it was the resulting panic that made California, and references to the Change Plague, the butt of jokes. All it seemed to take were a handful of self-infected fools to bring the entire state to its knees. The mere hint that a Changed was loose in a city caused officials to shut the city down.

That sort of idiotic overreaction created the meme of mocking anyone who even implied that the Change Plague was a problem. Unfortunately in Canada it all-too-quickly did become a serious issue. By that point, however, people were so afraid of being tagged as "Californian" that they just shut up and carried on.

The Canadian media certainly didn't help. In truth, though,

they were mostly owned and controlled by American interests and filled with stories from the American news feeds. As a cost-saving measure, you understand. Reporting on local events or issues was kept to a minimum— again in the interests of saving money. The longer that went on, the more people simply accepted that as the normal way of things and went on with their lives. Still, the speed of the acceptance was a bit strange, now that I thought about it.

The computer warbled a tune that indicated the analysis was done. Once again I stepped through the data overlain on the map. As before, the infections started in Toronto and radiated out. Curiously, the radiated infections roughly followed the US-Canada border. There were a few incursions into the US, although those all seemed to be earlier forms of the Change Plague.

Even more interestingly, those incursions seemed to be located at specific spots in the US—California, the Southwest states, and some of the Eastern seaboard. Nothing about that made any sense, and I just sat there chanting curses at the screen as I toggled through the displays again and again.

Suddenly it hit me—those were major industrial areas, for the most part. The handful of other infection points corresponded to transportation hubs. That helped to explain why the US was experiencing problems out of proportion to the number and type of werewolves. Well, that and the fact that their government officials tended to fly into a panic of security theatre at the least hint of a threat.

So, what about Canada? I ran another analysis of the Canadian data using a somewhat finer grid. Those results showed a similar pattern—the infections were targeting population and transportation hubs. The difference between us and the States was that we got all the most recent Change Plagues, we got more outbreaks of werewolves, and we got them first.

Lucky us.

So what did it all mean, besides the obvious? There was more to this, and I sat there trying to tease out the patterns and implications that I was missing.

OK, there was someone making a series of plagues and releasing them to specific areas. What could the vector of infection be? I decided to set that issue aside for the moment as something outside my expertise. Canada, and particularly around Toronto, seemed to be targeted for the most and worst of it. I couldn't think of any reason for that, and reluctantly set that aside for later consideration.

On the other hand, that precision targeting meant excellent intelligence. Could it also mean a small operation trying to make the most out of limited resources? Possibly, although it could also mean a large operation trying to fly under the radar until the time was right for a big strike.

Now wasn't that a cheery thought?

Wait a minute, though. This was obviously a long-term plan, and played to wearing down the social structure of the target countries. Yeah, but, how did the mere presence of the Changed cause such disruption to the social structures of Canada and the US? Or the rest of the world, for that matter?

That got me thinking about Europe. They got hit after they tried to reinforce economic ties with North America just after the first outbreaks. With the result that the EU turned its attentions inward and away from the larger world.

There were also rumours about attacks by the Changed in both Russia and China. Those occurred shortly after they really began ramping up their anti-Western propaganda. That propaganda became much more muted as they, too, became more inward-looking. This increased trend to isolationism did have one useful aspect, however. There were a lot fewer wars and peacekeeping situations around the world. So much so that most countries were scaling back their military expenditures—if only to deal with the worsening economic situation.

Which meant that someone was trying to isolate us, as well as destroy us. And yet ... was "destroy" the proper word? Perhaps "softening up" might be a better description. Or—and this thought gave me chills—perhaps we were being made ready for something.

Speaking of which it was time to save all my analysis work

and make backups. Then put together a summary of what I'd found, and put it into the email queue to be sent out to The Group whenever communications became available again. Maybe I had made a mistake in the analysis. Maybe my conclusions were wrong. It was time for other eyes to look at it.

Putting all those happy thoughts off to one side, I performed the backup rituals. While waiting for those to be completed, a small voice in the back of my head insisted that I'd missed something. Or rather, forgot to explore something. Frowning at the computer as it chugged away, I managed to tease out a hint for my disquiet. Something about the infection curves.

Poking at the curves for each year, I finally got to the last one when it hit me. This last infection curve was the right shape, but its origin was not in the usual spot. It seemed to start just as the last Plague finished, with no pause for winter. Which made no sense, because that would mean the infections should have started a lot earlier.

Which, in turn, meant we should have been seeing werewolves during the winter. Except that no-one did. On the other hand, there was a much larger than normal number of them around earlier in the spring. That implied infections, and werewolves, that no-one saw.

If something didn't make sense, then a useful rule of thumb was to look at it from a different point of view. OK, the infection curves dealt with the creation of the Changed. Perhaps a different way of looking at it could be found in the reported deaths of them. They died off every winter, so maybe the data had numbers on the bodies found?

A quick search showed that there were, indeed, yearly counts of deaths of the Changed. Despite the data being more than a little spotty, it was easy enough to do a quick plot of the number of dead versus the month they were found. I did that for every year in the database.

Then I overlaid the plots for all years onto a single graph. They all seemed similar, with no deaths seen until about May, reaching a maximum about December, and dropping to zero again in January.

Except for this last year. Like the others it slowly crept up from May, maxed out at roughly half the maximum of previous years, before dropping to zero in October. That made no sense, since the number of live werewolves seen was higher than normal, even into the fall.

Oh. Shit.

That meant that not only were there more werewolves than normal, there were fewer observed deaths. Added to the earlier-than-normal creation of werewolves, the inescapable conclusion was that a large number of them probably didn't die off over this last winter. Well, shit on a stick. This was ... disconcerting, to say the least.

But if no-one saw them all winter, where the hell did they go?

Speaking of which, why was Toronto reporting a much reduced number of werewolves this year? The last few years had gotten increasingly bad for werewolf attacks, but this year it was almost as if they weren't there. Why was that?

My weariness, temporarily put aside by this new analysis, returned in full force. Time to call it a night. I created a quick report for The Group—more of an addendum, really—and added it to the message queue. No need for a further backup since I'd just done that for the data, and I wasn't in any mental shape to do anything except go to bed.

With a sigh, I gave a stretch, leaned back in the chair, and closed my eyes for just a second to give them a rest before heading off to bed.

CHAPTER SIX
Night Sweats

I awoke with a start, and the clock showed I'd slept for nearly an hour. Worse, it was late at night and I hadn't made a security check in many hours. Not a smart thing to do, 'cuz that's when the werewolves were most active. Time to give myself a shake—both literally and mentally—and get back to the here and now business of staying alive.

I rolled the chair down to the security station and stared at the monitors. The automatics were supposed to let me know if anything strange occurred, although it was based on a simple set of logic rules, not an AI. A brief flash of movement caught my eye on one of the monitors, but there was nothing there when I focused my attention on it. A minute later, there was another brief flash of movement on another monitor.

Oh, those clever little monsters.

They'd learnt—the hard way—that my motion-detection algorithms were blind to brief movements followed by a long interval of no movement. It was a filter I'd programmed in to ignore blowing leaves and such. The trick now was to figure out exactly where they were before I enabled any countermeasures.

The night was too warm for the IR cameras to work well, but I switched them on anyway. I began cranking up the sensitivity of the regular cameras to see if I could spot anything, although it was too dark for them to be of much use.

The IR spot-sensors near the barn again flickered

intermittently. The IR cameras weren't seeing anything because of the latent heat in the ground. The regular cameras weren't showing anything useful.

I pushed those thoughts aside to focus on the issue at hand. The real question was, did this signal an attack or not?

Why was that important? The non-lethal countermeasures were something I preferred to use as rarely as possible, as the more they got used the less effective they became. That's why I normally kept the outside lights off at night.

There were intermittent readings from the spot-sensors at the front and sides of the house, although the video feeds still showed zilch. Whatever was happening was becoming more wide-spread.

OK, this was decision time. The only effective countermeasures were the strobe lights and sirens. There was also the new set of infrasonic generators I'd built a few weeks ago, but they hadn't yet had a live test. Sounds between fourteen to seventeen Hertz tended to instill feelings of dread and panic in people. Chimneys resonating at that frequency were the basis for reports of ghosts in old buildings. What I didn't know, was if it was going to have any effect on the werewolves.

As I sat there pondering options, I began to see more frequent brief flashes of movement. That settled it—it was time to put the fear of me into them. I made sure the video feeds were being recorded, and the high-resolution cameras ready to go as soon as the strobes started firing. Next, I turned on the infrasonics. The speakers began blanketing the areas around the house and barn with the signal.

All the various sensors indicated bursts of motion that ceased after a few seconds. As an experiment, I decided to add a dose of ultrasonics to the mix. These generators broadcast a random warbling sound well above the normal range of human hearing. Although not effective in the past, it was worth trying in case things had changed. To my surprise, a few of the intermittent signals became strong and constant as they moved away from the yard. Interesting, although it only affected a small number of the attackers.

Time to stop farting around.

I activated the automatic non-lethal defences, and enabled the anti-personnel weapons. These consisted of shotgun shells in metal tubes that functioned like mines, and were triggered automatically if something got too close. Some of these were tied into the security cameras, and some used a crude proximity sensor. The mixture of technologies and techniques made for a more robust system.

Setting the lights and sirens to go off in sixty seconds would give me time to run upstairs, grab a rifle, and snipe at targets exposed by the lights. I stood up, activated the timer, and ran up the stairs to the attic. The rifles there were all set to go with extra magazines, so all I had to do was to grab one, chamber a round, and start shooting.

Mentally counting down as I ran, I got to the attic with a handful of seconds to spare. Puffing slightly, I grabbed two rifles, chambered rounds into each, set the safety on one and put it on the floor next to me, and kept the other in my hand. The floodlights came on as the sirens began to wail. I poked the rifle out through one of the many available slots and scanned the front yard.

There were at least a half dozen figures that I could see, some frozen in a squatting position and others running away. I took out the runners first, then the squatters. My rifle clicked empty as I shot at the last squatter, who was beginning to turn and run away. Damn shame to have to let it go. I placed the rifle on the floor and picked up its sibling. Running to the wall facing the barn, I clicked off the safety, and scanned the area around the barn before firing at the few targets that I could spot as they ran away.

That's when the howling started—hunting howls. That was not good. That was very not good.

A quick scan of the security feeds in the attic showed all clear. I took the opportunity to slap fresh magazines into the two rifles I'd been firing. I also took the opportunity to prep and place a rifle at each of the four walls in the attic. That gave me five, counting the one in my hand. The coast was still clear and the security monitor showed that a few of the shotgun mines had been triggered. Those were all in the blind areas around the barn that I couldn't see from the attic. Enough of the mines remained that I wasn't too worried, despite those hunting howls. Enabling the rifle's safety, I put it on the floor, then hurried to the basement.

It was time to take things to the next level.

I strode to the control console, and set up the system to trigger the high intensity lights. These were a series of million lumen LED lights that I'd rigged up under the eavestroughs of the house and barn. They could be programmed to strobe individually, strobe as part of a pattern, or stay constantly on. Brighter than the sun, those bad boys could do serious damage to eyes even through closed eyelids. I decided to use the standard programs that I'd set up, and grabbed the remote control for them as I went back up the stairs.

As I got to the door I turned around and went back to the console and took a look at the IR video feeds. There were a series of faint blobs just at the limit of their effective range, which was a couple dozen metres past the fence. It almost looked like they were massing, and on more than one front. Upon seeing that I flipped up a safety cover and activated the mortars. These were manually activated only, and I transferred their control to the remote box I held. That was the full extent of my resources, and I once again went back upstairs. I paused in the kitchen to grab a couple of containers of water in case I got thirsty. Kipling was correct when he penned "But if it comes to slaughter, you will do your work on water. An' you'll lick the bloomin' boots of 'im that's got it". Especially the part about slaughtering.

Back in the attic, I confirmed the location of the rifles as I entered the room. After taking a deep breath to ready myself, I disabled the infrasonic and ultrasonic generators and turned off the floodlights. Using the remote control box, I set the high intensity lights to the dazzle pattern, which would strobe them individually in a quasi-random rotating pattern that would hopefully be disorientating. I set the intensity of the lights to thirty percent. Painfully bright, although not damaging. A wounded animal became even more dangerous.

I hoped to blunt the attack while I sniped at them from the attic. They had charged me like this twice before, though never on multiple fronts. And never after already being chased off.

I got my rifle, and went to the wall facing the front yard. They seemed to be massing there. I waited and tried to control my ragged breathing. After a couple of minutes of listening to the hunting howls, a warble from the security console alerted me to movement from the road. I peeked through the slot and saw maybe a dozen, more or less, running towards the house. A pair of slightly different warbles indicated a mass charge from two other directions.

After ducking, I activated all sonic generators and the dazzler program at the same time. The shrieking of the sirens was deafening, and I hurriedly dug out the ear plugs that I'd forgotten to put in. They brought the noise level down to something tolerable for me. A glance at the security console showed that two of the three lines had halted, with one of them starting to retreat.

The third, the one coming towards the house from the direction of the barn, was still moving. I activated the mortars for that area, and turned the intensity of the LED's up to sixty percent. The mortar shells, which were essentially small pipe bombs rigged with fins and a firing mechanism and propelled by emptied shotgun shells, began to rain down and fill the area with shrapnel. I thought I could hear screams of pain over the sirens. I wasn't sure, and didn't make an effort to listen. Once the mortars were done, I killed the lights and audio, then went to the wall-slot facing the road. I shot at a few werewolves milling about in the yard just off the road, and watched the rest scatter.

The security console indicated nothing moving. I toggled the console to show the IR camera feeds, saw only a series of cooling blobs. The attack seemed to be over. I waited another hour in the attic, sipping on the water. The security sensors showed no movement, and the cooling blobs became the same temperature as the ground.

None of my sensors, nor a visual check through the rifle's scope, could detect any trace of the wolves. At this point I made everything safe and racked all the rifles—I'd clean them out later. I went down to the basement where the full security console was, and did a complete and thorough check of the area. Everything was clear, without even a flicker on any of the sensors. Most of the antipersonnel shells had fired, and would need replacing.

I didn't bother to turn on the lights to view the battlefield. I knew what I'd see, and I wanted to put off seeing it for as long as I could. Come the morning, I'd be cleaning up the results of this night's foul work.

For now, I put the security system into automatic, disabled the mortars, sat back in my chair and tried to get some rest. I set some classical music to playing, and turned up the volume in an attempt to chase away the bleak thoughts rattling around inside my head.

Sleep would escape me, but I needed to get some sort of rest before facing the horrid chore awaiting me.

CHAPTER SEVEN
The Morning After

I awoke stiff and sore to the sound of a gentle trilling. Springing to my feet I dashed over to the control console before I realized that it wasn't the security system screaming for attention, just incoming email. According to the time displayed on the monitor, it was almost seven. It was uncommon to get emails so early in the morning after getting a bunch the previous day.

They turned to be emails from The Group, each flagged as "urgent". Each of them was roughly the same—each person asking me if I was alright after the big attacks. That puzzled me, as I hadn't told anyone about the events of last night.

The email from Stan offered a few more details. It turns out that there had been a couple of savage attacks reported on the outskirts of Toronto, but none in downtown itself. In fact, early reports indicated a sudden decrease in the already-sparse werewolf population within the city.

Interesting, and could explain the higher-than-normal numbers of werewolves I'd been seeing lately. I gave my head a shake. This wasn't the time for analysis. There was too much to do.

A quick glance at the security displays showed that all was quiet. The video feeds showed many bodies on the ground. My mouth tightened and my stomach clenched at the thought of the cleanup chore awaiting me.

The first thing to do, though, was to send a quick email to

The Group. I assured them that I was unscathed, gave a brief summary of the attack, and promised to send details after the cleanup. Was pretty sure they'd be able to figure out what I meant by the latter.

I sat staring at the array of monitors for a minute without really seeing anything. Giving myself a shake, I levered my stiff body out of the chair. It was time to do a quick security walk around the inside of the house before going outside. I grabbed the remote control console (a re-purposed netbook computer) and headed upstairs. At the kitchen I unplugged the slow cooker that I'd forgotten about, and put the pot of now-ruined stew on the stove to cool. The sight of the stew made me somewhat nauseous, so I sipped on some water before continuing my rounds.

Realizing that I wasn't at the top of my game, I did everything by the numbers. I checked the shotgun racked by the kitchen door, and ensured that both the inner and outer doors were locked and bolted. Drawing my revolver, I made sure that it had a round ready before proceeding through the rest of the house. I took care to check the windows (all long-since shuttered on a permanent basis), every outside door (locked and bolted), and every gun rack.

In the attic I took the time to refill each magazine from the boxes of cartridges stored there, and left a message on the whiteboard on the door reminding me to bring up more boxes of cartridges. I'd started to depend on leaving little notes to myself at the best of times, and these most certainly were not the best of times. Part of my mind noted that my handwriting was even worse than normal.

After making the rounds, I returned to my bedroom and changed into light cotton clothes. The old clothes were left heaped by the bed to be dealt with later.

A quick glance at the console showed that everything was still quiet, and bodies seemingly undisturbed. If the surviving werewolves hadn't used the bodies as a food source, they were probably nowhere near me. On the other hand, maybe the bodies I couldn't see had been scavenged. With a deep sigh, I realized that I'd find out soon enough.

I walked slowly down to the kitchen. The temperature outside was on the cool side, so I replaced my usual sneakers with heavy work boots, and donned a warm coat. Using a netbook as a remote console , I made a careful survey of all the video feeds and proximity sensors. Everything was still quiet. Some of the proximity sensors indicated something nearby, but the IR sensors indicated that those were all at ground temperature. In other words, corpses. Lovely.

Next, I went to the gun rack and took a shotgun, ensured it was loaded and had the safety on, then slung it. Taking another shotgun, I racked a shell into the firing chamber, and kept it in my hand. It was time to perform the exit rituals to go outside.

Once outside, I did a careful check of the exterior of the house by walking along the porch that surrounded the house on all four sides. It was a certainty that some of them would be watching me from hiding. It was important to be seen as an alpha predator patrolling my territory. I cradled the shotgun as I carefully walked the perimeter. Not too quickly and not too slowly, with as much self-assurance as I could project.

The other reason for my patrol was to check for damage to my defences. This was the first time that I'd fired the mortar rounds in anger, and I worried that the shrapnel (old nails and screws) might have damaged the house. It turned out that my calculations and tests had been spot on. The damage had been limited to the odd bit of metal sticking out of the wood.

I kept a wary eye out for any sign of hostiles as I prowled the perimeter. If the damned werewolves had broken the truce, I couldn't count on their old patterns of behaviour holding. With a start, I realized that the truce had only been an illusion. They had been biding their time, building up their numbers and casing the joint. Hopefully the events of last night convinced them to keep outside the boundaries for a while. And I had to stop thinking of it as a truce.

That got me to thinking. If they were breaking patterns of behaviour, perhaps it was time for me to do the same. I had always circled the porch in a clockwise fashion. So, when I got back to the kitchen door I reversed direction and did another casual prowl around the perimeter. Nothing out of the ordinary occurred, but it couldn't hurt to enforce the idea that my habits weren't as predictable as once believed. Predators typically disliked unpredictability, as it interfered with successful hunts.

Back at the kitchen door I stopped to do another brief scan of the area before heading down the stairs and over to the barn. I wouldn't be doing a circuit around the barn on foot—it was time to get mechanized. Walking over to the barn, I unlocked the door and entered. A quiet series of tones as I entered indicated that the security system was not detecting any problems. I shut the door behind me and the bolts slammed back to their normal positions.

I walked over to the security console, and performed a detailed check to verify what I'd seen from the house. As expected, the local system displayed the same information that had been relayed to the main system in the house—it never hurt to check those things.

The first thing that I did was replace the spent shotgun shells used in the antipersonnel mines. These were a short length of pipe that acted as a short-barrel shotgun, and electrically fired. The short length gave a wide dispersal pattern when the shells—filled with No. 4 buck—were blown. Exactly what was required.

After first engaging the safety switch at the console, I started replacing spent charges. As I pulled back each pipe to reload, I slid another precut sheet of thin plywood over the hole in the wall to replace the damaged one. Replaceable gun ports, in effect. With that completed, I went back to the security console and did a systems check of the mine circuitry. Everything seemed fine, so I brought the system back on-line.

That left the mortar rounds to replace. Those always scared the crap out of me, quite frankly. They were actually pipe bombs, fired out of their tube using a shotgun shell as the propellant. Their triggering mechanism would activate the bomb either on impact or after a period of a few seconds, whichever came first. I didn't have a lot of black powder, only enough for a half-dozen shells. I had rigged up four tubes, test-fired a few dummy rounds and one live round. Quite the fascinating technical project to be sure, but I soon realized that any friction or wind or what-not would affect the drop-point of those bombs. Definitely last-ditch weapons, but they had proved their worth last night.

With those cheery thoughts rolling around my head, I carefully replaced the spent rounds with the two remaining ones. Truth be told, I had never expected to need the mortars at all. Now it looked like I was going to have to revisit the whole idea of defensive strategies, and sooner than later.

Fucking werewolves.

With the essentials now taken care of, there were no more excuses to put off the task I'd been dreading. Oh, wait—a bio-break and a sip of water was as good an excuse as any. So was having my legs go weak. That required me to brace myself against a bench until the weakness passed.

Finally there were no more excuses.

I trudged off to the garage section of the barn, walking past the too-seldom-used tools that I'd so lovingly accumulated. What had been the painting area was now a sort of airlock between the barn and the garage. Or, rather, a security portal and storage area for smaller gear like snow blowers. It allowed me to keep the garage open without compromising the security of the barn as a whole. The garage itself was now sectioned off, with one vehicle per section. One section held the tractor, one section held the pickup truck, and each had its own garage door. When a vehicle was out in use I could, in theory, keep the garage door open, and there was no hiding spot inside and the portal doors were secure.

For the cleanup of the bodies I decided to use the tractor and its front-end scoop. I had enclosed and lightly armoured the cab of the tractor, and added a few sharp edges here and there to discourage anyone from jumping on. Certainly not a tank, but it could function as a light attack vehicle if needed.

Right now I was going to use it as a way of collecting the bodies for disposal without exposing myself to any attack. I hopped up into the cab, and slid the shotguns into their holsters within the cab. With those secured, I started up the tractor and gave it a minute to warm up while I checked its systems. The WiFi link to the security system was working well, and I took the opportunity to confirm that no problems had been detected. All systems were go, the engine sounded fine, the portal doors were locked, and the on-board cameras were feeding to the security system for recording. It was time to get to work. The garage door clacked noisily as I signalled it to open.

For my first pass I decided to go around the barn, to get a close-up view of the sides that couldn't be seen directly from the house. There would be some bodies there anyway. The tractor rumbled out slowly, and I made a sharp left-hand turn to approach the side. Turning the corner, I inhaled sharply. The anti-personnel rounds had done their job effectively. There were at least four bodies.

I lowered the scoop and began cleaning up the carnage. Luck was on my side—it only took one pass to get it all. I drove up to the burn-pit about thirty metres away, and halted just at the lip. Dumping my gruesome load, I slowly panned the scoop back and forth over the remains to ensure that the cameras could make a good record of them. That might be useful data at some point.

When finished, I used the scoop to drop a layer of scrap wood over the bodies. I backed up to another group of bodies, and repeated the process of dump, scan, and cover with wood. The process was repeated again. And again. And again.

I had been surprised not to see any of the mortar casualties when I walked to the barn. Turned out that there weren't many complete bodies. Those, plus lots of shredded chunks, lay within the grass that grew along the driveway. The grass was just over a foot high. From the placement of the bodies, it appeared that some of them had crawled through it on their bellies. That was new behaviour and would explain the intermittent IR sensor readings, as the grass would help mask their heat. The mud that covered some of them also probably helped to mask the IR. The mud was new behaviour, too, as they tended to keep themselves fairly clean. There was no significant standing water on my property, so the mud must have come from elsewhere.

New tactics, more awareness of sensors, and a willingness to stand their ground in the face of light-and-sound repellents all boded ill for my future safety. I stopped to write myself a note to get rid of all the grass between the house and the fence. My hands were shaking so badly that the note was illegible.

Enough stalling—I put the tractor into gear, lowered the scoop, and made a careful sweep of the area to clean up the remains. Some probably got missed, but the bulk of it ended up in the scoop. A trip to the burn-pit completed the disposal process.

The next area requiring cleanup was the front yard. The bodies there were mostly intact, at least on the side the bullet had entered. My soft-nosed hunting rounds made for pretty gruesome exit wounds.

There were six bodies for the dozen shots I'd fired. A satisfying ratio, since I was quite sure that some had dragged themselves away, if the bloody smears on the lawn and across the road were any indication. Blood loss of that magnitude would have killed a normal human, but the werewolves gained a measure of enhanced healing from the Change Plague. Even so, if they survived it would be some time before they could be a threat to me again.

The bodies filled the scoop more that it was designed for, but I was determined to be done with this horrid task. I headed back to the burn-pit as gently as I could, so as not to spill anything. Reaching it without incident, I dumped in the bodies, taking care to get a video record of them.

The pile now reached the edge of the pit, making it hard to pretend that out of sight meant out of mind.

With the last of the bodies dumped and covered, came the tough part. I headed back to garage, grabbed a sack of paraffin bricks and a couple containers of kerosene, before heading back to the pit. I unsheathed one of the shotguns, unlocked the door, and stepped outside. There was nothing in sight, but it was important to reinforce the habits of caution.

I slung the shotgun, then scattered chunks of paraffin on top of the pile. The kerosene was poured over as much of the wood as possible. Finally, I took a couple of road flares from out of the tractor cab. After lighting, I tossed them onto the kerosene-soaked wood. Climbing back into the cab, I watched the fire. As the flames spread throughout the pyre, I offered up a short prayer for the souls of the departed and wished them peace.

Look, I hated werewolves as much as the next person, but each one of them was once a human being. It was highly doubtful that they acquired the Change Plague by choice, so those poor bastards weren't at fault for anything their Changed forms did. Some of the dead looked kind of small, and I truly hoped it was just because they were small adults.

Sometimes hope was all we had.

After watching for a minute or two, I put the tractor into gear and headed back to the garage. It was time to wash out the scoop and get on with other chores that waited for me. No rest for the damned.

★ ★ ★

Cleaning out the scoop involved spraying it first with water and detergent, then steam. There was a lot of nasty stuff still sticking to it and starting to dry. It took me the better part of an hour to finish the job and clean up the area. All the ooky bits got collected in a bin for later disposal in the fire pit. Jolly good fun was had by all. I only puked twice—though hard enough to make my chest ache.

I was feeling somewhat woozy by the end of it, and it took me a minute to realize that a large part of that was because I'd been doing a lot of work but had eaten nothing for over fifteen hours. I took a minute to sit down and sip at some water, and nibble at one of the protein bars I always kept on hand in the barn. The house was my main base of operations, but the barn could be used as a secondary base if need be and had enough supplies for a week.

After eating half of the protein bar I carefully put the remainder in a resealable bag and put it into the barn's fridge. Waste not, want not. I took a couple more sips of the water before tossing the rest into the sink and rinsing out the cup. Always leave your workplace clean at the end of your shift.

Focus on the mundane. One foot in front of the other.

Before I went back to the house, I took a security walk inside the barn, starting with the upper sniper nest. Using the binoculars I scanned the area, but could see nothing amiss. Looking over at my neighbours' houses I could see the green signal lights gleaming. Either they had beaten off the attacks, or the werewolves had only attacked my place.

Which was possible, actually, since I'd been the sole target of attack a few times. It was comforting to see that my neighbours were OK; I wasn't sure that they could have beaten off an attack like the one I just experienced. Or maybe they could have, through sheer volume of fire.

My head was beginning to ache, so I decided to take some joy in my neighbours' good fortune, and carry on with my rounds. After putting the binos in their slot, I climbed down to the main floor. I checked that the garage door was locked and bolted, collected the shotguns, and prepared to head back to the house. The security system indicated nothing of note, so I slung the one shotgun and held the other at the ready as I unbolted and opened the door.

Stepping out, I did a cursory scan around and headed back to the house without incident. The sound of the bolts slamming home to secure the door sounded like a gunshot and I jumped a bit. Once inside, I racked the guns, and hung up my jacket. Whoops—forgot to eject the shell in the magazine. With a shake of my head, I did that and double-checked that the safety on each shotgun was engaged. This was no time to slack off on proper safety.

My headache was getting worse, and I was feeling overall draggy. Time to make myself a cup of tea. While I waited for the water to boil, I grabbed a bun from the container. It was a few days old, but would still be edible.

After the water boiled I dropped a tea bag into a cup and poured in the water. While the tea steeped, I took off the heavy work boots and put on my sneakers, leaving the boots sitting on the floor outside the closet.

Those could be dealt with later.

I figured that I should head on down to the basement, look at the videos of the bodies, and document what new breed of horror had attacked me. I took the teabag out of the cup and dropped it into the sink, to be dealt with later. Slipping the bun into my shirt pocket, I headed downstairs carrying my cup of tea.

My headache was turning into the stabbing-of-needles-behind-the-eyes kind, and made me feel a little nauseous.

Walking down the stairs I stumbled a couple of times, slopping hot tea and scalding my hand. There were wet spots of tea on the stairs but I left them to be dealt with later. Transferring the hot cup to my uninjured hand, I blew on the burned hand as I entered the room and sat down in front of the main console. I took a careful sip of the tea, grimaced at the heat of it. Taking the bun out of my pocket, I took a small bite before placing it down next to the cup. My hands were still shaking a bit.

Hesitating for a moment, I called up the video recordings taken earlier. The past couple of years had seen increasing body changes, and I was curious to see what this new crop of werewolves might be like. I scanned through the videos of the first lot of bodies, pausing only to save the odd frame that had a usable view. It appeared that this lot had been hunched over as they walked. Their heads had been at the same level as the shotgun blasts. Messy.

Many of them had a thick layer of mud over their entire body. Interesting. I wondered if it was an attempt to stay warm, or an attempt at camouflage. I doubted the latter, as that would assume a degree of planning and cognition that no-one had ever seen in the Changed.

The recording reached the point where I had dumped subsequent groups into the pit, and I paid careful attention to try and catch a better glimpse of bare limbs or an unruined face. There were some useful examples of both.

It looked like the shape of the face was now altered into something resembling a short muzzle. The teeth were definitely less human than expected. As well, the proportions of the limbs seemed strange—though that would take careful measurements to confirm.

My headache was getting worse again. I paused to take a couple of sips of tea, which by this time was on the cool side. My eyes were drawn to the security cameras that showed the fire pit. The fire had consumed enough that the mound was now below ground level. The flickering flames cast a ghastly light show in the gathering gloom. Sparks rose up on the thermals created by the heat and drifted away out of sight.

Far, far away from the horrors in the here and now.

No more guilt, no more pain.

I reluctantly turned from that and returned to my study of a group of bodies that had been ravaged and shredded by the mortars. These showed rather more extensive changes to the hands and limbs. The few intact faces were certainly more bestial in appearance. There were fewer mud-caked pieces, although that could be attributed to the force of the blast.

The images of the final lot of bodies were the most disturbing. These were the old-type of Changed, the most human-like in appearance—extreme hairiness notwithstanding. Interestingly, they were all naked. Dirty enough, to be sure, but not covered in mud like the other two groups. I sorted the accumulated pictures and filed them away in a dated folder, with a few brief notes of the attack and my observations of the remains.

As I finished that, the room spun about me. This continued long enough that I had to grab onto the arms of the chair to steady myself. I took several deep breaths and tried to calm myself.

They were only werewolves. They had tried to kill me, as they had killed so many others. It was self-defence.

The pain in my head was almost blinding by this point, and I climbed to my feet and tried to walk. After a few steps my legs gave out and I fell to my hands and knees.

They were werewolves, I kept telling myself, and they were on the hunt with me as their target. For years they had hunted me. They had kept me isolated from my friends. They were werewolves. It was self-defence.

I tried to get up again, but the room was spinning all around me. I stumbled and fell onto my side.

They were werewolves, but my mind kept seeing them as men and women. That I had killed. Burned their bodies to erase all memory of their existence, as I had erased their lives.

It was self-defence. It was a war of survival.

My head was spinning and pounding, and I began sobbing uncontrollably.

Men and women, who through no fault of their own had been turned into monsters. Monsters that I had been forced to destroy. To kill and kill and kill.

The sobbing turned into screams as emotions ripped through and out of me. Or rather, I tried to scream but my chest felt caught in a vise, and all that came out were anguished wheezings and moans.

The vomiting began shortly thereafter. Perhaps it was an attempt by my body to purge the horror I had kept bottled up inside me. For years.

Eventually, oblivion claimed me.

CHAPTER EIGHT
Harsh Realities

I woke up feeling cold, wet, and drained. My throat was raw. My head felt thick and my thoughts slow.

Every sphincter had let loose when my stomach emptied itself. I was covered in various forms of human waste, both outside and inside my clothes. I could hear soft musical alerts being played by the computer system.

Ignoring those, I levered myself to my feet and stood upright. That was a mistake, and I was forced to hunch over with my hands on my knees until the spinning stopped. Eventually it did, and I carefully stood upright. Glancing at the control consoles I saw no flashing red signals, and there was no hooting of the alarms. That meant there was nothing that wouldn't keep while I pulled myself together.

The only thing that I could focus on was the need for a shower, although the idea of hot water seemed vaguely nauseating. I stumbled towards the stairs, each step an exercise in ignoring the squishing sounds and the feel of cold, wet clothing. I stumbled my way upstairs to the shower stall.

Turning on the water, I stepped in and gradually increased the temperature. Every so often I would get the dry heaves. I ended up curled up at the bottom of the shower, trembling as the hot water blasted me. Eventually I regained enough composure to strip off my clothes, hanging them on one of the hooks inside the shower so that they wouldn't block the drain. After that accomplishment, I slowly and carefully scrubbed every square inch of my body, several times.

I held my face up to the water and let it scour the inside of my mouth and as much of my throat as I could tolerate. Coughing and spluttering I got the inside of my mouth clean enough to be merely foul-tasting, which was a huge improvement. I stayed there until the hot water run out. After that, I stepped out and began to dry myself. Every movement required a great effort, as if I were swimming in molasses. My throat still hurt rather a lot, but was tolerable.

I lurched into the bedroom to put on underwear and socks, followed by a tee shirt and a warm flannel shirt. A chill around my legs caused me to realize that I had forgotten pants. I hurriedly grabbed some sweatpants and put those on. Something still didn't feel right—then I realized that I wasn't wearing my belt with its usual assortment of attachments. Important stuff like my revolver.

Crap.

I walked over to the shower, and sure enough my belt was still on my soiled pants. With the revolver and various other sundries on the belt. Not having the energy to curse anymore, I simply removed the belt and its attached devices and dropped the pants to the bottom of the shower. I'd deal with the mess later.

I grabbed a towel and placed each item removed from the belt upon it. The only things that worried me were the revolver and electronic gadgets. Despite having spares, I needed to salvage those.

About all I could manage now, however, was to put everything on a dry towel. After a moment's consideration, I took the pistol and emptied out the cartridges, leaving them on the towel with the revolver opened up. This would have to do for now, though it would need a good cleaning later.

It was time to try and get myself back into shape. There was work to do—like staying alive in a world trying to kill me. To be honest, it was a real effort to care about that.

The first order of business was nourishment of some sort, although the thought of food didn't sit too well with me. Broth, I decided—a light broth was what was needed. I went down to the kitchen, selected one of the few remaining packages of instant broth from the pantry, and set the water to boiling.

While that was going on I checked the security readouts (something I should have done after getting out of the shower), and was gratified to see that everything appeared to be clear. The video feed from the front of the house even showed no werewolves on the road, which was rare. I needed access to the full security console in the basement to do a proper scan. Although right now what I really needed was to eat something before I keeled over from lack of nourishment.

After the water boiled, I prepared the cup of instant soup and sat at the small kitchen table to drink it. I sipped slowly, and it seemed to settle my stomach nicely. On the assumption that my stomach was queasy due to being empty, I decided to risk eating a couple of crackers. My throat was too raw to handle them dry, so I chewed them well and washed each mouthful down with a bit of the soup. The warmth felt soothing on my throat despite the residual rawness.

The small meal had done wonders to clear my head and settle my stomach. I stood up carefully and felt no dizziness or weakness—which I took as a promising sign. Now it was time to go downstairs and check the various systems thoroughly. As I was leaving, I turned to the pantry and grabbed a roll of paper towels. Normally I liked to conserve those, but just this once I couldn't be bothered to be thrifty.

I walked slowly down the stairs, holding onto the railing with one hand for support. Walking into the basement, I stepped quickly off to one side to avoid the trail of bodily fluids on the floor. I tore off paper towels to cover the trail, as well as the large pool where I had lain unconscious for hours. Suddenly I remembered that I'd have to clean up the trail of nastiness leading up to my bedroom. Shaking my head with a sigh, I promised myself that I'd get around to it later.

That was getting to be a bad habit, leaving things for later. Too much of that and you'd create a pile of work that seemed insurmountable to even attempt to do, and so you stopped trying. I'd been down that route before, and didn't want to revisit it.

I froze into a state of indecision broken only when a musical trilling came from the console. That was the focus I needed to kick my mental processes into work mode. First things first. Deal with the demands of the external world, then worry about the home fires. With priorities established, I tossed a few more paper towels onto the mess before going to the console to see what was happening.

As the alerts had indicated, it was a series of emails from The Group. They'd been sending them twice an hour for the past several hours, and the subject headers showed an increasing level of concern for me. I opened them up and my initial impression was confirmed. When I hadn't sent any more emails, they'd gotten concerned. More so after getting no response for so many hours.

I typed out a quick note to all, explaining that I'd had an attack of jitters after the cleanup and that everything was fine and that more details would be forthcoming in an hour or so.

Not really a lie, just a more severe attack of jitters than I wanted to let on. Right now I needed to gather together the photos of the attacking werewolves, and expand on my notes on how the attack unfolded. Jitters, or PTSD, or whatever it was could damn well wait—something new was happening and my friends needed to know about that. The first task was to send the latest photos and notes to everyone in The Group.

With that message sent, the next task was to figure out how to deal with the latest analysis without getting Dixon into trouble. I decided to refer to it as a re-analysis of our existing data. If Dix wanted The Group to know more, he could tell them. That data was not just sensitive, it was probably seriously Top Secret stuff even these days. With that decided, I needed to arrange the graphs with appropriate annotations and associated notes.

Ordinarily I'd use R's knittr or some other reproducible data tool to produce an integrated code plus data plus results type of report. This time, however, I decided to focus just on the results. No sense in tempting the fates, since several of this lot were of the type to want original data and code to verify things for themselves. I was in process of deciding what graphs to use and how to annotate them when the system announced the arrival of another message from someone in The Group.

I leaned over to see what it was, and smiled as I saw that it was from Lee. She and I had worked together for a number of years, and she was a trusted friend. I opened up the email, and sighed as I read it. She had read between the lines, and strongly suspected that my "attack of jitters" was rather more than that. She was tactfully wondering if I'd been on a massive drunk.

She always worried that living alone led to severe alcohol abuse problems, and never quite believed me when I denied it. Getting tipsy once in a while was not abuse. Getting blind stinking drunk, now, was abuse. Something I hadn't done in a decade or more. After a bit of soul-searching, I composed a message thanking her for her concern and assured her that it wasn't due to drink. It had been something of an emotional meltdown and please don't tell anyone else, and more data will be on the way Real Soon Now, so let me work. I sent the email, and knew that she wouldn't tell anyone. She was somewhat overly protective, but could keep a confidence.

With that taken care of, I got back to work.

I decided to keep the results of the analysis simple. First, the final chart, showing how the Change Plague seemed to be a series of new plagues each year. Also, a chart showing the progress of Ebola outbreaks, flu, and measles. Those would show the curves for standard diseases and highlight that the Change Plague was a series of plagues. Combine that with the pictures of the Changed from the most recent attack, and it seemed quite clear that these plagues weren't the result of random variations of the original virus.

If it wasn't a natural phenomenon, then someone was making it happen. That was an ugly thought, yet one that I needed to throw out there for The Group to look at. I wasn't sure what any of us could actually do about it, but they'd have all the information I had—or at least the analysis thereof.

After about twenty minutes of work, I had the annotated graphs, a brief explanation of what the regular disease outbreak curves meant, and what I thought the analysis of the Change Plague data meant. I collected them all into a single compressed file and sent it out to them.

With that done, I turned my attention to more mundane matters. I had a nasty series of messes to clean up and laundry to do. One step after the other—there was no time for an old man's weakness.

CHAPTER NINE
New Beginnings

It took the rest of the morning and much of the afternoon to catch up on chores. By the end of it my mental equilibrium was back—more or less. The biomess was all cleaned up and disinfected (had to watch the health issues), the guns were all cleaned, ammo replenished, the kitchen cleaned, and a full security walk around of the house (inside and out) done. By the time I was ready to do the security walk, I had changed into my regular clothes and was wearing a proper belt with the usual set of weapons and paraphernalia.

I was glad to see that there was still no sight of any werewolves anywhere near my property. The battle seemed to have rattled them even more than I'd hoped.

Which reminded me, I needed to think of some new ways to both discourage and stop any future attacks.

I'd had a few thoughts on that a few years ago when designing my defences, so the first step in that direction would be to read those notes again. The next step would be to take into account how much things had changed for the worse.

The black powder used for the mortar shells, for example, was now almost gone. It was unlikely that I'd be able to get more, any time soon. Besides, mortars were rather too omnidirectional for my liking.

I decided to put off planning issues until after supper, in favour of more immediate issues. If nothing else, I needed to do some mindfulness exercises to help get my head straight.

The thought of the last battle and the grisly cleanup still sent shivers down my spine and made my legs feel a bit wobbly. I'd killed a few werewolves before, of course. And had come across corpses after they had died of natural causes. The fire pit was built to take care of those few instances—rotting bodies were bad for the health, all in all.

There were two important differences this time. The first was the sheer number of bodies—I'd never been attacked by, or killed, so many. As for cleaning up, after the few previous attacks the bodies were in short order either gone or torn apart and unrecognizable. Similarly for the bodies I had stumbled across. It's a hard world out there, and protein was protein for a hungry animal.

On top of that, the small stature of some of those bodies tore at my soul. I'd never seen children among the Changed. The Plague always killed the few of them that became infected, from everything I'd heard. Maybe the new form of the virus was keeping some of them alive. Or, with any luck, they were just small adults.

Those thoughts caused my head to swirl. I had to spend several minutes working on my mindfulness mantras until I felt fully in control of myself again. It wasn't calmness I was striving for—rather, alertness without being tense.

With the basics taken care of, I decided that now would be a dandy time to cut the grass that the werewolves had used to such good effect during the attack. I wasn't sure what to do about it other than cut it and keep it cut, although that would be a good first step. That task would require me to head out to the barn, which would give me an opportunity to confirm that I'd locked it down properly after the cleanup. Also, I wanted to spend some time surveying the area from the sniper nest.

Before heading out, I gathered up a few boxes of cartridges to take with me. Always best to not go empty-handed when it might save a trip later. I also decided to take along a spare shotgun and revolver to leave at the barn, to boost the armoury stock there.

The lack of werewolves was beginning to pique my interest as something that needed a closer look. None of the security sensors could detect anything, and I wondered just how far they had run. I also wanted to check the security signal lights of my neighbours, and cursed the phone and broadband lines that seemed to be down on a permanent basis.

The trip to the barn was made without incident. After catching myself breathing a sigh of relief when the bolts slammed home behind me, I snorted amusement at the show of nerves. The first task was to put the spare guns and ammunition in their appropriate storage areas. After that, it was a toss-up whether to go to the sniper nest first or cut the grass, but I decided that cutting the grass was the immediate priority.

I slung the shotgun and went to the garage section that housed the tractor. Cutting the grass involved replacing the front scoop with the lawn-cutting attachment. A straight-forward task that took me a lot longer to complete than it should have.

Once done, I closed and secured the door to the barn, climbed into the cab of the tractor, slid the shotgun into its holster in the cab, and started up the tractor. Everything seemed to be working fine, and the remote security readouts showed no problems. I signalled the garage door to open, and as soon as the door rose I eased my way outside, taking a careful look around.

After ensuring that everything looked OK, I turned left and headed for the grassy strip between the house and the fence. The grass cutter made a one and a half metre swathe. The grass strip was about twelve metres wide by thirty metres long. So allowing for overlap, that would take twelve passes and the better part of an hour to complete.

It ended up taking somewhat more than the expected time, what with swerving around a few roses and slowing to be extra vigilant the closer I got to the road and fence. I had a few queasy moments when the mower went over some of the bloody bits that I'd missed. Fortunately, those moments passed quickly enough.

It was late afternoon, and the sun was not too far from the horizon, when I finished the cutting and was parked back in the barn. It took me half an hour to remove the grass cutter from the tractor, and hose everything off. Never leave your tools in a dirty state—they'll work better and last a lot longer. After a bit of thought, I decided to re-attach the scoop. It could be used as a fearsome weapon, and I was beginning to think in terms of *when* the next attack might occur, not *if*.

I re-entered the barn proper, leaving the lights on in the garage. This wasn't something that I normally did, but I wanted to break up my routine. Keeping the shotgun slung, I went upstairs to the sniper nest for a look-see. Racking the shotgun, I picked up the binoculars and did a quick scan.

That showed nothing of interest, so I did another scan taking care to pay particular attention to the wood lot areas, looking for any shapes or shadows that might indicate a werewolf. It occurred to me that I was going to have to get to those wood lots to cut wood for next year's stock. Rather than worrying about that right now, I wrote a memo to myself in my notebook to look into it later, then promptly erased it from my mind. It was better to write notes than trying to remember everything—that just wasted mental energy.

There didn't seem to be any hostile activity near me, nor in any of the fields or woodlots. I turned my attention further afield to my neighbours' houses. All three of them showed green on their security signal lights, and each had lights on in some of the windows. I could only see the rear of their houses from here, and everything seemed to be as intact and tidy as it ever got. They never took security measures as seriously as I thought they should, and simply smiled indulgently when I lectured them about it.

Maisie Frontenac—her family lived in the house closest to mine—would take the opportunity to hand me some cookies and a cup of tea. She always insisted that the authorities had everything well in hand, that they were fine, and that I was just worrying too much.

Come to think of it, though, when I first broached the idea of the signal lights everyone thought it was a damn fine idea. Even took the time and dollars to get them installed. Worked pretty well for a while, too, especially when the phone lines went out. Over the last year or so, people seemed to just sort of settle back into their old ways. More so since this last winter.

Perhaps I was over-thinking it all.

Newcomer city folks like myself were, at best, tolerated by the locals who had multi-generational roots in their communities and often on the same plot of land. Before moving here I'd heard some bad stories regarding newcomers moving to the country, but my neighbours were really quite welcoming. Oh, sure, there was a bit of distance at first. Everyone loosened up when they realized that I wasn't going to stop their kids from raiding the fruit trees along the border of our properties, or get upset when their livestock wandered onto my property. Old Phillip got a little miffed when he found me trying to teach his wandering cow to play fetch. Or maybe it was because the cow was starting to do it.

It helped a lot that I was more than willing to leave the actual farming stuff to them, and happily bought the fruits of their labour. I overlooked the fact that I was paying top dollar for it. It was great quality, fresh, and quite frankly they needed the sales and I could afford it.

My own farming was limited to some vegetable gardening for use by my friends and myself, I was content to let the overworked land heal itself. The only other things I planted were herbs and flowers suitable for the bees. The locals loved that I had all sorts of flowering plants and let them keep their hives on my land in exchange for some of the honey. The bees were good for their crops, and I got a real kick out of helping out. Bees were cool.

The Frontenacs, Maisie and her husband Brandon, were the ones who had broken the ice and made sure that the other neighbours knew who I was. After first making sure that I wasn't some idiot city asshole, of course. Which was more than fair. They were umpteenth-generation farm kids and managed to make their little farm pay for itself, more or less, and had been trying for the past year or so to make their own crop of new farmers. Almost five months ago they ecstatically informed everyone that Maisie was preggers.

A couple of weeks ago Brandon had done his first planting. It was a little early for that sort of thing, although the mild weather ensured that the ground was ready. On top of that, Brandon wanted to try and get a jump on the competition to maybe squeeze in an extra planting of something or other. Those kids had great instincts, but I had to wonder if now was the time to be bringing children into the world. However, they had a farmer's optimism, and neither they nor their neighbours had had as much problem with werewolves as I had. My own theory was that the frequent roar of the large farm machinery kept the wolves off balance, and so they focused on easier prey.

Me, for example.

Brandon and the other farmers swore that shotgun shells filled with birdshot were enough to keep the buggers away. Old Philip swore by rock salt. I tried both of those, but found they only worked for the first year or so. Heck, I wouldn't even have had a shotgun—or a gun of any sort—if Brandon hadn't insisted that I needed one in case the coyotes and wild dogs came prowling around.

Later, the werewolves started becoming more numerous. Even started coming right up to the house some nights. That's when I began building up my armoury. I also set up my security systems, and added various non-lethal defences.

That worked well for a season. The year after that, however, they began prowling around my house both night and day. That's when I killed my first, although it wasn't the last. Killing one or two of them a year seemed enough to convince them to stay away, and I managed to harden myself to that.

I'd kept the fact that I'd killed a few over the years a secret, as the vicious brutes still looked far too human for the comfort of most people. At first I worried about the police. After a couple of years, though, they began to stay close to the villages and left the farms alone unless a farmer's death was involved. Don't ask, don't tell.

Anyway, no-one had believed me when I suggested that the werewolves came after me preferentially, so I stopped talking about it and just dealt with things as they occurred. I would normally keep to myself in the winters at the best of times, and kept in touch with the neighbours by phone and the odd email. The roads would become treacherous or even impassible, and I refused to get a snowmobile on account of I hated the damned noisy things with a passion.

This last winter was the same, except that the increasingly unreliable phone lines made the usual calls all but impossible, and I sort of lost touch with neighbours. The increased presence of the damned werewolves on the roads made travel impossible for me, and I assumed for the others as well. What with Net Nights, emails, and the occasional voice contact via ham radio, my need for human contact—never terribly strong—was satisfied.

Even so, they were my neighbours and I should be doing a better job of looking out for them. I don't think they would have understood about plague curves and genetic alterations, though. Still, maybe it was time to put them into the loop for all that, whether they laughed at me or not.

With a determined snort I lifted the binoculars to my eyes and looked towards the Frontenac house. Everything seemed fine, and nothing was out of place, but it all seemed too quiet. Suddenly there was movement in the windows. There were human-shaped shadows against the closed blinds, occasionally moving from room to room. I let out a breath that I wasn't aware that I'd been holding. A check of the other houses showed similar activity as evidenced by shadows on the drawn curtains. Well, it certainly looked like everything was OK with them.

Maybe the werewolves kept away from the others because of a memory of the "big noisy beasts" that prowled those lands. The snowmobiles and large farm machinery scared me, that's for sure.

I glanced at the clock and decided to call it a day and head back to the house for supper.

★ ★ ★

After returning to the house I had a light supper of a cheese sandwich with tea. It went down easily and stayed down without complaint, and was surprisingly all I wanted. Although a lot better than it had been earlier in the day, my throat was still tender. After finishing the tea, I made myself another cup.

This time a melange of lemon mint and a few other dried herbs from my garden.

I grabbed a couple of cookies for snacking, and headed downstairs. Time to hit the emails and check in with The Group. For some reason I felt the need to reach out to my friends.

My footsteps were light and steady as I descended to the basement, and I didn't need to use the railing to support myself. I decided to accept that as a promising sign that I was recovered from my emotional trauma. Entering the basement and glancing at the monitors showed me that there were, indeed, emails waiting for me. With a sense of eagerness, I sat down and began to examine my bounty. After a quick glance, though, a disgruntled sigh escaped my lips.

Spam. The world was coming to an end. My link to the outside world was a tenuous low-bandwidth satellite link, and my inbox was filled with spam. Sigh.

Refusing to let such trivialities bring down my mood, I took a deep cleansing breath and forced a smile to my lips. With my calm suitably enhanced, I carefully examined the contents of each email. After a dozen deletions, the email program finally scrolled to the point where I could see some emails from members of The Group. There were, alas, a handful of spam emails between me and them. I maintained discipline and read each email in turn before consigning it to the bit bucket (that's the electronic garbage can, for the digitally illiterate).

The first real email was from Gail. She asked me how I was doing ("Goddammit, Lee," I muttered), and assured me that Lee was blameless except for not changing the password on her home computer. And anyway she was worried about me.

Sigh. I liked Gail a lot, but she had a problem with the concept of personal space when she worried about a friend. Still, she was the sort of big-hearted free spirit that it was impossible to stay angry with, tempted as I was to try. Reading the rest of her lengthy email dispelled any negative thoughts.

Gail worked at the Royal Ontario Museum as a forensic anthropologist. She had taken a detailed look at the photos I'd sent of the latest werewolves, and had some interesting observations. After lamenting the lack of a specimen to study (and apologizing for perhaps being insensitive), she said that there appeared to be three different classes of werewolves from the attack.

The first group resembled the victims of the Change Plague from a couple of years ago.

The second group, representative of most of the remains (for what it was worth), resembled the werewolves first seen last autumn. The third group was new, and wasn't yet reported anywhere else that she was aware of. These seemed to be overall stockier in build, with distinct muzzles, mostly non-human style of teeth, and feet suggestive of elongated paws rather than human feet. As well, the limb proportions were all wrong for humans. The legs, especially, gave her pause until she realized that the knees might be backwards-facing, like a dog's. Or maybe a strangely-constructed joint, or maybe just a damaged joint. It was hard to tell for sure from the pictures.

She went on to say that the mud coating the new-style werewolves was not dissimilar to that seen in some primitive tribes. It was sometimes used as protection from the elements, and sometimes as an element of rituals. The idea of a ritualistic element was bolstered by the description of the attack as being done by separate but coordinated group. The pictures I'd sent showed not just groups of new-werewolves, but new-werewolves as part of a group of old-werewolves. That might indicate that the new-werewolves acted as leaders or shamans that the old-style werewolves would follow.

I flopped back in the chair as the implications of her words hit me. It was bad enough that the new-werewolves, as she called them, were able to hunt effectively in large groups. Now she was suggesting that maybe the new-werewolves could bend the earlier versions to their will. That would be double-plus un-good. Hell, that would be ultra-mega un-good. I gave my head a shake, and bent forward to read the rest of her email.

Despite the limited information provided by the pictures, if her conclusions about the leg-joint orientation were correct perhaps the new-werewolves would be as comfortable in a four-legged gait as a two-legged gait. There had been unsubstantiated sightings of more bestial werewolves floating about for several years, which no-one paid any attention to. However, after seeing this latest batch of pictures she was prepared to give some credence to those reports.

After that, she switched to a more personal tone. "Holy moley, Felix, where did you get that analysis about the Plague being new plagues each year? Oh, by the way, Lee has something to say about that, though I'll let her tell that story in her own words."

Well, that was interesting. I drank some of the now-cool tea and nibbled on a cookie as I tried to take in what Gail had written. An uber-werewolf, able to control the lesser breeds. Yeah, that summed up what the data seemed to show. On the other hand, it was a single group, from a single attack. A large attack, to be sure, but a single attack. Yet on the other-other hand, to even mount a large attack of that sort would seem to bolster the uber-werewolf theory, wouldn't it?

Gahh! I scrubbed at my face with my hands and decided to put all that on the back burner while I looked at the other emails.

Suddenly the security system warbled for attention, though with a "this is interesting and not normal" chirp, not the "holy shit look at this" siren. Sliding the chair over to the security section of the table, I quickly scanned for the cause of the alert. Nothing was immediately evident until I looked at a seldom used part of the system and saw the cause—the audio sensors. The system had picked up on some unfamiliar sounds outside. I didn't usually bother listening to the outside microphones. After the first few, werewolf howls were not terribly interesting. This time, what I heard after turning on the speakers made my blood ran cold.

The werewolves were howling in a new and utterly non-human way. It certainly wasn't their hunting cry. Maybe it was an identification, or a summons. Whatever it meant, it was loud and insistent.

I sat listening to it for a minute or so before turning it off. Piss on 'em. It was tempting to respond to that howl with my own set of sonic generators. After a bit of thought I decided not to, as it might suggest that I was responding to them. No, I was the alpha predator and would ignore them. With luck, that's how they would interpret it.

After a moment's consideration, I armed the various non-lethal defence systems. After a moment of sober second thought, I armed the anti-personnel mines as well. Just in case. Turning off the speakers, I went back to my emails.

There were a couple of emails from others in The Group thanking me for my last analysis and situational update. They offered their best wishes, and promised to get back to me as soon as they had a chance to digest and think upon it. Normal stuff, and just what I needed.

Nothing from Dixon, though I wasn't concerned about that. If I knew him, he would be sitting back with a smug smile. At the next face-to-face meeting, whenever that occurred, he would drop hints about the source of my data, as was his wont. A smart kid—I'd leave that decision up to him.

The next email was from Lee, and after a quick scan I gave my head a shake and went back to read it carefully from the beginning. She was an assistant curator at the ROM, and typically dealt with sorting through and cataloguing ancient artifacts that arrived. She only had a bachelors degree, which limited her formal career possibilities. However, her near encyclopedic knowledge and computer skills made her a highly valued member of the team. So much so that she had quickly reached the top of her pay scale, and then some. Her bosses tended to give her unprecedented freedom to do her own research, so long as her regular work got done. If only more employers were so enlightened, I thought bitterly to myself before focusing on the matter at hand.

It seems that the graph of the plague curves had caught her eye. They closely matched the ornamentation on some very old artifacts that the ROM had recently acquired. The series of curves for the Change Plague matched almost exactly an ornate symbol on a couple of the artifacts. Almost, except that they showed one more cycle of plague, and that in turn was tied to a symbol for destruction or catastrophe. An alternate interpretation for the symbol was "Armageddon".

Lee went on to add that the artifacts were from a little-known pre-Sumerian civilization. It was not even known what they had called themselves, so archaeologists had merely assigned a code. Later civilizations knew of it and made passing references to it, or so the experts believed. Sketchy as they were, all the references were remarkably consistent. They spoke of a powerful kingdom and the rise of a great evil that laid waste to it. The only names assigned to that kingdom translated to "the damned" or "the accursed". Ornamentation that matched the plague curves was found in two separate later civilizations, with specific references to that lost kingdom.

The last part of her email said that the project supervisor, Professor Manderpootz, was one of the few experts in that lost kingdom and she would confer with him. It was probably nothing, but strange enough to bear looking into.

I didn't know what to think after going through that. My usual store of profanity failed me. After a moment's consideration, I ate the cookie and washed it down with the now-cold tea. Then I gave my head a shake and decided to finish reading the emails. What else could I do?

The last email was from Jack. Well, actually Jack and Clio. There was never the one without the other, even though they'd been married for a few years. Clio had a friend who was an economist with one of the big banks. It seems that countries untouched by the Change Plague—like the smaller Asian nations and the Middle East—had decided to officially shift their trade to South America, the only other large area unaffected by the Change Plague. It would be taking affect gradually over the coming months. North America and Europe were going to become more and more isolated as time went on. The news wasn't yet widely known, yet, so I should treat it as confidential for the moment.

Oh, lovely, I thought. Just what our already shaky social and economic structures needed. Travel in or out the affected areas had been increasingly discouraged for a few years, and was now to the point where special permits were required by most of the unaffected countries. The EU made the mistake of emphasizing travel tourism a couple of years ago. It was an unaffected zone at the time, needed the money, and medical opinion was that the risks were low. Turned out that medical opinion was wrong, and the Change Plague hit there soon after the tourists did. That pretty much put an end to tourism everywhere. The only travel being done these days was by sealed cargo vessels, and it looked like even that sort of thing was about to dry up. Once word of that got out, an economic crash was a near certainty. A crash that would make any previous economic crash seem minor in comparison.

This could become the end of civilization as we knew it—the Long Night.

This was beyond not good.

A vague numbness seemed to settle in my brain, which I shook off as best I could. I composed a short summary of how I was doing. I mentioned mowing the lawn to prevent more sneak attacks, that my supplies were fine, and that the gardens were growing well. After a moment's hesitation, I mentioned the new howling that had started that evening. I recorded a minute's worth of it and appended the audio file to the message, in case it might mean something to someone. After sending the email to everyone I decided to call it a night.

My dreams that night were troubled, and my sleep not at all restful.

CHAPTER TEN
The Gathering Storm

When I woke up from my unsettled sleep, it was still dark outside. Glancing at the clock I could see that it was an hour before my usual wakeup time. I decided to get up anyway, and went through the usual morning rituals.

A check of the security console in the bedroom showed that everything was clear and there had been no alerts during the night. After getting dressed, I went downstairs for caffeine and nourishment—with emphasis on the former.

Entering the kitchen, I set up the coffee to brew and set some water to boil for porridge. It's trite, but true, that breakfast was the most important meal of the day. While waiting for everything to get ready, I decided to take a brief peek at the main console in the basement. The remote consoles were adequate, albeit limited. So many things to improve, and so little time.

I hustled to the basement, moving with quick ease down the stairs, keeping one hand lightly on the railing. Rather than sitting, I leaned on the edge of the desk to scan the various displays. The security logs showed that last night's howling had ended about an hour after it started. Interesting—that might be something useful to track, to see if it correlated with anything.

The communications console was less encouraging, as it showed that the satellite link had become increasingly intermittent overnight, and was now down. The phone lines and cable TV were still down, which wasn't much of a surprise.

Oh, well. It looked like I'd be in for a few isolation days. That would force me to focus, that's for sure. I went back upstairs and commenced to feeding the inner man.

★ ★ ★

While eating breakfast I came up with a rough schedule for the next little while. I'd put data analysis and worrying about the Change Plague on the back-burner for a bit, and focus on hardening my defences. After cleaning up, I sat down with paper and pencil. Writing things down always helped to focus my mind.

If these new type of werewolves were going to be taking things up to the next level, I'd have to prepare for that. That meant the first task would be to review the physical security of the house and barn. The greenhouse was a weak point for sure, and I needed to deal with that somehow. All that glass made it a difficult area to harden. It might help to widen the beds of garlic and wolfsbane outside of it, and to plant more roses. Barbed wire was of limited effectiveness, as I had found out the hard way, and besides I had no more of it.

What I really needed was razor wire, but that had been in short supply for a few years because it was allocated to hospitals and other essential government facilities. The remainder got snapped up for industrial security, leaving none for individuals. There were equivalents that I could make, though until now it hadn't seemed to be worth the bother. The main problem was that anything along that line worked only when there wasn't any snow covering it, and the winters were damn long and severe. On the other hand, once built they were always there. All in all, improved passive defences of some sort were worth looking at in more detail, so I put them at the top of the list.

The next big thing had to be weapons. The OPP, like all the police, frowned on people taking direct action on their own. The local cops were reasonably tolerant about allowing non-lethal self-defence (unlike the Toronto cops). However, they would come down hard on even the hint of "crazy American-style militia survivalist bullshit" as they liked to call it when they lectured me. At length, and more than once—although they never caught me doing anything illegal.

Unfortunately, things had progressed beyond the point of worrying about what the police might think. I needed something to take care of those massed waves used during the last attack. Some sort of area-denial weapon, like mines. At a minimum, I had to defend the perimeter of the house and the barn, plus have layers of these mines so that I could take care of several waves of attacks. That added up to a lot of mines. Maybe cannons of some sort would do the trick. In either case, the question was how to implement them with what little I had on hand. So that got on the list with a big star beside it.

Somewhere on that list had to be communications. I needed to somehow get more reliable communications with The Group and my immediate neighbours. It would also be a fine idea to contact the local OPP detachment. Unfortunately, with the phone lines down it was impossible to contact them. They used to monitor CB channel 9 up until a few years ago when budget cutbacks put a stop to that, although maybe they had started that up again. Not that it was of any use, of course, as I had no CB radios. Ham radio gear, sure, but the local OPP didn't go in for that sort of thing. I wrote "communications" on my list with a big question mark next to it.

Next was power, though it got placed at the bottom of the page. That was something that I'd set up years ago, as much for fun as with an eye to the future. For emergency backup power, I had a bank of batteries that, in theory, should be able to supply a full power load for a week or so without any charging. If I reduced my power consumption to the bare minimum (that is, fridge and freezers), that could stretch to almost three weeks. To keep the batteries charged up, I had solar panels, wind generators, a propane-powered generator, and a couple of generators powered by steam and Stirling engines. The entire system got a good workout several times a year, and had never failed to make a smooth changeover. With power so flakey these past few months, the main parts of the system had gotten a good workout. Just in case, though, maybe checking the seldom-used generators should be closer to the top of the list than the bottom, as I hadn't done that for several months.

The final item I came up with was food. I had three freezers stocked with meat, plus a large basement pantry with tinned and dry goods. There was a large supply of flour, beans, and rice stored in five-gallon cans which I'd flushed with nitrogen before sealing to eliminate the chance of spoiling. All in all, I was in excellent shape for food, so long as I didn't mind a bland diet when the fancy foods were gone. However, recent events had brought home the real possibility that I was going to be on my own for food sooner than later. My gardens would help an awful lot with that, and give more than enough to divert towards my friends.

That pretty much summed up, in broad strokes, everything that I could think of. It occurred to me that checking my inventory of stuff might not be a bad idea. That had the advantage of double-checking what I thought I had, act as a sanity-check in case I'd forgotten something, and might help spark some useful ideas. Along those lines, I decided to check out the stocks of building materials in the barn first.

When I'd first moved up here, before the Change Plague bullshit, I loved using the various tools to make stuff. With more enthusiasm than talent, I had a lot of fun. Even managed to help my neighbours with their farm equipment, now and again. Many of the gears in their tractors, for example, were made of plastic. If those broke, replacements cost far too much and never lasted as long as the original piece. I would take the original and use that to make a mould and cast a new gear or adaptor or whatever in aluminum or steel. Sometimes I'd just carve something out on the CNC mill or lathe if they could come up with the raw stock. Great fun and a great way to interact with neighbours—and get yummy food in return.

Giving my head a shake to focus on the here-and-now, I kitted myself up for a trip outside and went out to the barn. I took a look around on the ground floor and re-familiarized myself with the stock available to me. There was some irrigation pipe that I stored outside, but I didn't bother with that for the time being. Right now I was more concerned with lengths of scrap iron, how many nails and screws of various types were on hand, and what sorts of lumber I had.

It turned out that I had forgotten how much of all that stuff I had accumulated over the years. I'd always hated to throw stuff away. Nothing sparked creativity better than a well-stocked junk pile.

After that pleasant interlude, I went upstairs and poked about the office. I needed to ensure that the computer with the CAD software worked. The next big task would be to start up and test all the machinery downstairs, but that was a task for another day.

With a sigh I realized that I was putting off the task of doing the outside survey. Chiding myself for being foolish, I went up to the turret, grabbed the binoculars, and began a methodical sweep. I began with the grounds around my house, then gradually spiralled outward. Everything seemed quiet, and I didn't catch sight of any werewolves.

My lips tightened as I began looking that the Frontenac house. Spying on my neighbours just seemed terribly wrong. The security lights still showed green, and I could see the occasional shadow pass in front of the closed curtains. Odd. Maisie always made a point of drawing the curtains each morning. To "let the day in", as she would cheerfully say.

Another oddity was the lack of activity in their fields and around their barn. Well, perhaps I had just caught them between work periods, or maybe they were under the weather or something. I still felt guilty about not getting in touch with them sooner, despite knowing full well that circumstances had been preventing that. With an unhappy sigh I pushed my unease to one side and examined the homes of my other neighbours. They all seemed fine. I had to assume that if something were wrong, one of them would have indicated it.

With the inventory and survey completed, I decided to head back to the house. Upon returning, I stored everything back in its proper spot and made myself some lunch. After washing the few dirty dishes, I headed to the basement to check out all the various systems.

The communications console showed that there were emails despite the satellite connection fluttering up and down. A welcome development, indeed, and I sat down to read through them. Some were spam, some were newsletters, and one was from Lee.

I deleted the spam, then opened the email from Lee. She had been taking another look at the pictures of the new type of werewolf, and specifically the mud that they seemed to cover themselves with. There appeared to be symbols of various sorts scratched into the mud. They were difficult to see, so she had a go at enhancing the pictures—something she was quite proficient at.

There appeared to be three or four distinct symbols. She'd been forced to interpolate using pictures from several different bodies. Despite that, she was confident in the results. Surprisingly, the symbols looked similar to the ones on the pre-Sumerian artifacts that she had told me about the other day.

What's more, Professor Manderpootz had gotten wind of her little project, and came storming in to her office demanding to know what she was doing. He was very possessive of his research. After showing him the symbols she'd extrapolated from the pictures, he confirmed that they matched those found on the artifacts. She showed him the unprocessed pictures of the symbols in the mud coatings—explaining them away as photos from an old African expedition. That seemed to shut him up right away. He apparently just stood there with his mouth gaping open for a few moments, then dashed off muttering to himself. Such a strange man, she said. She promised to send more details when she managed to beat them out of Manderpootz. I wasn't entirely sure that she was joking about the beating part.

That unexpected bit of news rocked me back on my heels. This was getting seriously strange, as if humans genetically altered to become bestial horrors wasn't strange enough. I wanted to query her some more, but the satellite comms were down again. Just as well, perhaps. I needed to do some serious thinking about what this implied.

It occurred to me that we needed better labels for the different types of werewolves. Maybe something more descriptive than "new", "old", and "old with markings". The new batch had markings like shamans and led the others, so I decided to call them "Priests". That seemed to fit nicely as I rolled it over in my mind. As for the others that followed orders even unto death, well "Drone" seemed as apt a descriptive name as any. As for the Drones with markings, maybe "Ultimate Drone" or "Uber Drone" or something like that. Anyway, just separating them as Priests and Drones would be fine for practical purposes.

Whatever labels I gave them, it sounded like things could only get worse.

CHAPTER ELEVEN
Batten Down the Hatches

The next morning found me drinking coffee and drumming my fingers on the tabletop. I'd been pondering the question of defences and weaponry until late last night, until I decided that getting some rest might help.

There were lots of things that could conceivably be done, of course. The problem was the limits on my time and resources. It wasn't as if this was a new problem, historically speaking. The basic thing was to have a solid structure that could shrug off attacks by weapons or massed charges. That sort of thing was, after all, why castles were built.

My house and barn were damned sturdy, although built of wood and therefore not fireproof. However, I'd painted everything with a fire-resistant paint shortly after I bought the place. On the plus side, the werewolves didn't have any weapons and didn't use fire. So a sturdy wood structure should be fine.

In terms of passive defences, spikes were a historically-proven deterrent. The current versions—barbed wire and razor wire—were of limited effectiveness and availability. That left me with the idea of building real spikes of some sort. Maybe use lengths of 2x4s with nails or screws sticking out. I had lots of lumber, and a decent supply of nails and screws.

On the downside, such things could be neutralized by covering the spikes with something. Like the seemingly never-ending supply of Drones. Well, anything that would slow down their massed charges was a Good Thing. Making such goodies should be fairly easy, so that got put at the top of the list that I'd begun last night.

I paused for a moment, then add two sub-items to that—affixing boards with spikes to the house structure at various points around the outside, plus other boards that I could put out on the lawn and driveway. The problem with the latter was that they could be easily dragged away unless affixed to the ground. Quick-set concrete would take care of the attachment problem, so that got noted on the list.

It would be easy enough to make up some sort of semi-permanent thingie with spikes, using either metal or wood beams. Speaking of metal, it would probably be a sensible idea to make up some big, honkin' spikes with a flange to allow screwing onto a base or the side of the house or whatever. That would allow the creation of layers of spikes, with the big ones shielding the little ones. I had enough scrap to make up a few dozen of those, and more than enough acetylene and oxygen tanks to cut them up.

Thinking about spikes got me to thinking about caltrops. Used for hundreds of years, those nasty things could be tossed out to impale horse hooves, tires, or feet. Straightforward to make, if some sort of jig could be rigged up. They'd be even more effective if I could figure out a practical way to sprinkle them in front of a massed charge just as the charge occurred.

That pleasing thought put caltrops at the number-two spot on the list, with a sub-listing for a way to cover a large area with them quickly. If nothing else I could toss handfuls of them out a window, or rig boxes of them on the roof and dump them out by pulling on a rope.

All those ideas were fine and useful, but I wanted something with a little more punch to it, not to mention able to reach further out. Rifles had great distance, and shotguns had a wide spread at short distances. Unfortunately I had a limited supply of ammunition, and no way to get more. I needed something that could throw a slug of material out at as high a velocity as possible. Cannons came immediately to mind—unfortunately,

I had almost no black powder left.

There were a couple of potential solutions to this. One was the venerable potato cannon—take a tube that was closed at one end, spray in some hair spray, ignite hair spray with a spark plug, and *BOOM*.

Well, given my own lack of hair I didn't have any hair spray. Still, any flammable liquid would do. Maybe propane—I had lots of propane. The trick would be setting up hoses with appropriate safety valving so that the resulting explosion didn't blow flames back into the propane tank. The complexity got that idea put at the bottom of the page.

The other possibility was to use compressed air. Releasing it rapidly would be equivalent to an explosion, but unfortunately with considerably less energy.

On the other hand, it could be used to fire out the caltrops and broadcast them over a wide area. I had some air valves that, on paper, had a fast opening time. Perhaps it could fire out grape shot, a sort of shotgun-esque technique used to such devastating effect during the age of cannons. That tended to be hard on the cannon barrels, though. However, maybe I could get around that by holding the shot inside a cartridge that would blow away as soon as it left the barrel—a sabot type of thing. That all sounded like it could work, so it was put down as the third item on the list.

Another idea that occurred to me was to make some sort of flamethrower. There was something appealing about the thought of spraying an onrushing horde of werewolves with liquid fire. The really big problem here was what to use for fuel. I had some gasoline, though I'd prefer to use that for the generators and vehicles, thank you very much. Propane would be suitable for a short-range kind of flame, and easy enough to rig up. But, again, the problem was one of limited fuel. Might be worth making up a couple nozzles, or souping up one of the weed-burner nozzles I had laying about. On the other hand, fire was certainly a double-edged sword, capable of doing as much damage to the defender as the attacker. I put it down as the fourth entry on the list, but with a question mark next to it.

My coffee was quite cold by that point and I debated whether or not to refill my cup. I looked at the clock and decided against it. It was time to start making stuff.

★ ★ ★

The next few days were a flurry of activity. The first thing I did was to make up some spikes to attach at various locations around the house and barn. They'd make it damn dangerous for anyone to sneak around either building by hugging the walls. As deadly effective as the point defence cells were, they could only fire once. Sharpened spikes were a gift that kept on giving.

My final designs included a type with three spikes for corners, and another for mounting along walls. The spikes for each had a sharp point, and additionally I sharpened the edges to knife-like sharpness before welding everything together. That took most of one day. However, much of that time was spent doing prep work and making jigs, so subsequent production runs would go a lot more quickly.

I spent the rest of that day making up some lengths of 2x4's with spikes at various angles. At each end of the boards I attached a length of rebar, about the length of my forearm. Those could be used to quick-install the barriers by simply hammering them into the ground, or setting them in with some fast-drying concrete mix. I didn't have as much of that mix as I had hoped—only enough for two or three sets—which limited its use to essential areas, like the steps at the front of the house.

Before cleaning up, I dragged out some lengths of small-diameter metal rod that would be perfect for making caltrops. The spikes wouldn't have to be too long—maybe six to ten centimetres in length. All they had to do was penetrate the bare feet of the werewolves. I could cut them to length with either the cut-off saw or torch. Bending would be quick and easy, and rigging up a jig for welding was a simple matter of gluing some bits of wood together. Or I could use epoxy glue, if it came to that.

It was a fine start, and that ended the first day's work. It was late when I finished up, so after checking the security console I decided to call it a night.

The next day I spent a few hours cutting the metal rod up for caltrops. Initial calculations showed that for a spike length of six centimetres, each length of rod stock would give me a dozen caltrops. After using up a couple lengths of rod stock, I decided to shorten the spike length to get more out of each piece of my limited supply.

It occurred to me that I could even make use of some of the wire clothes hangers that I had. It wasn't the best quality metal, but adequate for what I wanted to do with it. I had some of those in the barn, so I cut up a couple and bonded them together with glue. The result wasn't too bad when the sharp end was cut to something approaching a needle point, and was a lot quicker to make than using the rod stock.

I spent the rest of the afternoon assembling caltrops, making up a mixture of heavy and light ones. With some of the leftover lengths of rod stock I fashioned caltrops with one longer spike. That would allow me to anchor it into the ground or a structure. It was a good day's work, and I decided to take a break for a decent supper before continuing for the night.

I had always enjoyed making stuff, and all this shop time was actually making me happy. Then I remembered what it was for, and some of that happy feeling vanished. That touch of sadness reminded me to stop for a break and check the security console more often.

After supper I checked the basement consoles, and found everything to be quiet. The satellite feed was still down because of yet another solar storm, so there were no more emails. Disappointing, but I had work to do so it didn't bother me too much. With a long-absent spring in my step I went back to the barn to work in the shop.

After making a good supply of caltrops I was somewhat stiff from the physical effort. Deciding it was time for something a bit more cerebral, I began to take a crack at designing an air-driven cannon of some sort. It was a trivial exercise to make a quick-and-dirty cannon—just take a length of pipe, close off one end, add an airline and valve near the closed end, and voila! Toss in your ammunition of choice, set the air pressure, quickly release the valve, and ⋆WHOOSH⋆.

The strength of the "whoosh" depended on the air pressure and how quickly the valve could be switched. Being able to control those variables was the difference between a proof of concept and a usable weapon. A manual valve was too slow, so obviously I was going to have to use an electrically-controlled valve. I had about a dozen of those in stock, left over from one of my crazy ideas that didn't work out from years ago. That limited the number of cannons I could make, so the next thing to do was choose a barrel. Well, that decision was affected by what sort of ammunition I was planning to use, and that in turn was affected by the type of tubing I had available. Damn, I loved engineering-type problems.

The tubing available was either metal in 1-inch diameter, or 2- and 6-inch PVC pipe. The metal pipe could take higher air pressures. On the other hand, the PVC pipe could take larger ammunition. The 6-inch would be best for scattering caltrops quickly over a wide area, so I tentatively allotted three valves for that. That could protect the front yard, driveway leading up to the barn, and the area between barn and house.

After a moment's consideration I decided to add another for the rear of the barn to prevent attacks coming from the fields. That hadn't happened yet, so it was damn sure to be coming. So, four valves for the 6-inch pipes to scatter caltrops, with the remaining eight valves to be used for the grapeshot rounds. On second thought, maybe just six for grapeshot and save two for solid shot. I needed to figure out the details of the grapeshot rounds, but I left that as a task for later.

As useful as the air-driven cannon concept was, it was a single-shot device that had to be manually reloaded—not optimal for a one-man defence. A usable first start, to be sure. Still, it would be really nice if I could figure out how to easily make up something allowing each cannon to fire several shots before reloading. I put that problem in the back of my mind as I started playing with bits of this and that while thinking of ways to make a grapeshot cartridge. If I was willing to live with a single shot, then I could fire the grapeshot right out of the barrel, without requiring a casing of any sort. OK, so maybe just have a whole bunch of single-use barrels and somehow feed the air to only one of them at a time. Something of a plumbing nightmare, even if it was feasible.

With no obvious solution springing to mind, I decided to call it a night and go back to the house. Once inside, I went to the main console for a final check. Although the satellite link was now working, the only email was spam.

A definite sign from the gods that it was time to go to bed.

CHAPTER TWELVE
The Storm Hits

My sleep was restful, and I awoke with the rapidly-fading memory of pleasant dreams. I got out of bed feeling refreshed and eager to face the day. It had been quite a while since I'd felt so happy in the morning. A hearty breakfast reinforced the positive feeling, and I headed out to the barn for another fun day in the shop. Werewolves or no, I was enjoying playing with tools and making stuff.

Arriving in the barn, I exchanged my jacket for a shop smock. It was time to build me some cannons. The answer to my quandary of last night had finally come to me. I realized that "best" was the enemy of "good enough", so single-shot cannons would be fine. That made things a lot simpler, and I could finish them off today.

I had arbitrarily decided that my barrel lengths should be one and a half metres. With luck, that would be long enough to give any ammunition a stable flight and short enough to be easy to mount. After cutting several lengths of pipe, I sealed one end of each, drilling a hole into the seal. The holes were used to mount an electrically-activated valve.

Taking break for a quick lunch, I began the process of mounting the cannons. That proved to be a time-consuming task, since I had to figure out where to put them, and how to attach them firmly. In addition, I had to worry about how to load them, and how to make a clear path for the ammunition to travel.

I decided to rough-mount them for the time being, then do a walk-through to see how the loading would work. It also gave me a chance to string the control wiring to the valves and run the air lines from each cannon to the air compressor system.

I had set up two of the cannons before realizing that they should all have been tested first. A rookie mistake caused by overeagerness. With a sigh, I returned all the cannons to the bench to make testing easier. Only one of them failed, which proved due to a loose wire in one of the valves. That's what testing was for, I reminded myself.

Mounting everything was tricky, since I needed the barrels to be solidly attached to something in addition to having a clear shot to the outside. The six-inch caltrop broadcasters I mounted upstairs pointing downward towards their respective fields of fire. The other cannons I mounted on the ground floor, a couple of metres off the ground, aimed slightly downward though holes that I drilled. They were medium-range weapons, not meant for close-up work.

Hooking up the control and air lines was straightforward, and proceeded without problems. I mounted the barrels such that I could slide them away from the wall, and braced the sides with a block of 4x4 wood so that it could fire without moving.

The control wires were strung into the local security control panel, and wired into spare input/output control lines. With the air pressure disabled, I made sure the control panel indicators could actually toggle the lines they were meant to, and also sense that the valves had air. Wonder of wonders, everything worked first time. That didn't happen often, so I accepted it as a gift from the Fates.

The question of ammunition was easier than I had initially thought. For the caltrop loads, I made up a loose cylinder from some thin cardboard stock, put the cylinder into the pipe, then dumped caltrops in to fill the cylinder. Being loosely folded, I expected that the cardboard cylinder would fly away as soon as it left the barrel, after fulfilling its task of easing the passage of the caltrops. I did a similar thing for the two-inch cannons, except those I filled with short screws and scraps of metal.

For solid shot, I had some ball bearings that were a perfect fit. To supplement those, I also cut some lengths of steel bar-stock. In all cases, I put in a bit of packing to hold the ammunition in place, and some clear plastic wrap over the open end of the barrels to keep them clean.

It was late afternoon when I finished. To make use of the remaining daylight, I decided to start mounting some of the spikes. Checking the security system to make sure that there were no threats, I tossed spikes and screws and a power screwdriver into some sacks, slung a shotgun, and went outside.

At each corner of the barn I put two of the corner spike sets, one just below knee level and the other at waist level. I placed the wall-spikes between the point defence cells. Going back inside to restock, I repeated the process for the house.

I headed back to the barn as the darkness began falling. After collecting a couple bags of caltrops to keep in the house, I locked up the barn, and went back to the house.

The idea of having some caltrops in the house pleased me. For one thing, I could toss them around inside if there was a danger of someone breaking in. For another, I could always toss them outside by hand.

As I walked outside towards the house, I paused and looked around with a sense of pride and contentment. Until, that is, I looked toward the road, and saw a werewolf squatting on the far side. He dashed off into the fields as soon as he saw me looking at him. That was enough to put an end to my happy mood, so I went inside and put everything away,

After a quick dinner I went downstairs to better monitor the security system, and to set up the control of the cannons. It was only the matter of an hour to integrate the new cannons into the defence system. A simple task, but it was gratifying to see the new weapons and air reservoir showing up on the control screens.

I kept an eye on the security monitors as I worked, otherwise things would have finished sooner. There were a couple of short howling sessions just before midnight, neither of which lasted more than a few minutes. Every so often I could catch a glimpse of something moving in the fields across the road. In the darkness it was impossible to say for sure what it was.

Despite watching carefully for over an hour, I saw no movement of any kind in the yard. That encouraged me to set the security system to flash the outside house lights if anything breached the perimeter, and do the full strobe-and-wail routine if anything got within a dozen metres of house or barn.

I decided to go bed a little earlier than normal, but kept my clothes and shoes on.

* * *

The next morning I awoke earlier than usual, and before sunrise. I got up and splashed water on my face, buckled on my weapons belt, and headed downstairs. Although the security readouts showed no problems, I still felt uneasy, through for no reason that I could put my finger on.

It was when the coffee started brewing that it hit me—the werewolves had changed their routine. I snorted amusement, and realized the irony of the situation. I probably had them disconcerted with my strange new ways over the past few days, and here I was getting worried about their changed behaviour. That thought made me chuckle.

After a cup of coffee and some cereal I felt a lot better, and began to plan out my day. The sun was just beginning to rise, and all was at peace. Suddenly, the security alarms went off and the outside sirens began their wailing. Hesitating slightly, I decided to go to the basement to get a better overall view of the attack, or whatever it was.

The basement consoles showed that there were, indeed, incursions by hostiles towards both the house and barn. These weren't massed attacks, though. Rather, dashes by single werewolves towards the house or barn, followed by running back to cover in the fields. That was new.

Wait. Not just new behaviour. Those were scouting runs. Designed to test out my defences after the changes I had made.

Bloody hell.

I turned off the outside lights and sirens and waited to see what might happen. As the sun rose I could see movement in the fields across the road, as evidenced by the tops of the grass moving. The movement stopped, and nothing else happened.

After some minutes of no movement, I went upstairs to the kitchen. Grabbing one of the bags of caltrops, I opened the front door, and tossed handfuls of them up and down the porch and down the stairs. When the bag was empty, I closed and bolted the door and ran back downstairs.

It was as if my brief dash outside was a signal. I heard a series of barks and howls, then several ranks of werewolves rose out of the grass and dashed towards the house. Each line of them was separated by several metres. They bypassed the front of the house and continued down the driveway towards the barn. They must have hoped to catch me out in the open.

I manually activated the strobes and sirens, and they slowed down to a halt as their heads lowered and their hands covered their ears. A few of their number rose up—Priests, from the looks of them—and started howling something. The Drones began to move forward again.

"Fuck this shit," I thought to myself, and triggered the cannons. First the grapeshot, followed a few seconds later by the caltrop-broadcasters.

It was a beautiful sight, as many Drones staggered to their knees howling in pain. Some tried to continue forward, stopping when they stepped on the caltrops and fell to the ground writhing. The Priests moved quickly to be in front of them, carefully stepping over the caltrops. Seeing that, I fired off the solid-shot cannons and the one grapeshot cannon I'd left in reserve. The Priests stumbled as the shot hit them, but they stayed on their feet.

I ran up to the attic, grabbed a rifle, and began firing. It was amazing to see how they ignored the caltrops in their feet when faced with bullets firing at them—they knew that guns killed. I was sure that I had hit several of them, although there were no bodies left behind. It was as if they took their injured and fallen away with them as they retreated. More new and unsettling behaviour.

As attacks went, this was nothing like anything that had come before. This was so organized and carefully executed, unlike the mob-like tactics they used previously. Realization struck me—this wasn't an attack, as such. This was a careful and deliberate probing of my defences. This was new, military-like, and very bad news.

I turned off all the lights and sirens, and scanned for hostiles. Nothing in sight, not anywhere on my property or in the fields as far as my cameras could see. Normally a loss like this would keep them away for days. But now?

A thought came that chilled me to the bone—what about my neighbours? I needed to check up on them. The phone lines were still dead. The satellite link was working again, and a list of emails blinked for attention. Those were going to have to wait. I needed to get to the sniper nest in the barn to check on my neighbours. Still, no matter how eager I was to do that, I needed to ensure my own safety.

A check of the security console confirmed that none of the point defence cells in the house or barn had fired. Yet more proof that the latest attack was a probe-in-force, not a real attack. The cameras showed no signs of activity.

Chewing on the inside of my cheek, I decided that it would probably be prudent to do a visual check from the attic. That wasn't something that I normally did, since the cameras and sniper nest did a better job, overall. However, the attic would give me a better view of the front of the house and the fields beyond.

So up I went to the attic and spent some time scanning the fields and roadway. It was those damn fields that a bothered me most, as the grass could hide an awful lot. There were also small woodlots scattered up and down the road between the fields. My concerns seemed unfounded, as I could see nothing of any werewolves. Which meant that I probably had the rest of the day to make ready.

Probably.

Maybe.

Things seemed quiet so I went downstairs, collected my gear, and went over to the barn.

The first thing that I did was to reload the cannons. I put a double load into half of the grapeshot cannons. That would probably be safe, though I couldn't be sure until it fired.

100

Reloading the cannons, re-arming their controls, and recharging the air pressure took the better part of an hour. I checked the security controls one more time to confirm that everything was clear before heading upstairs to the sniper nest.

I was puffing a bit by the time I got up there, and forced myself to sit down and wait until my breathing had evened out. Using the binoculars I did a careful scan of the area, paying special attention to the wood lots. I didn't see anything of interest there, so I focused my attention on the Frontenac house. Their security light was still glowing green, and nothing seemed out of place although the curtains were still drawn. I sat watching it for a couple of minutes and caught a glimpse of the occasional shadow on the curtains.

Lowering the binoculars, I sat starring out while drumming my fingers on the tabletop. Rubbing my hand across my mouth briefly, I exhaled sharply and put the binoculars away. Binoculars were all fine and dandy, but for the distances I was trying to see over I needed something with more optical power. Something with enough magnification to peer inside a window a kilometre away and make out faces. I went to one of the storage closets and brought out the powerful refractor telescope that I kept there.

This was a rude and intrusive invasion of my friend's privacy. As I set up the telescope on its sturdy stand, my hands were shaking a little. I was extremely uncomfortable peering into other people's private lives like this, but it had to be done. Within a few minutes, the telescope was set up and ready to use.

After pausing for a moment, I forced myself to look through the eyepiece. It took me a few seconds to align and focus it on the house. It popped into view as if I was only a few metres away. The back door was slightly ajar and there were some brownish stains extending down from the handle. The woodpile at the back was askew, too, with some of the wood scattered around the patio. That wasn't good.

I carefully slewed the telescope to view each window in turn. There was nothing untoward until I got to one of the upper story windows where the curtains were partially pulled open.

No-one could be seen. All the pictures on the walls were missing or askew. This was the guest bedroom, if I remembered rightly, and was always kept neat. Something was not right, but I had no proof other than a bit of messiness.

I repositioned the telescope to look more closely into the spare bedroom. It proved to be a mess, with the mattress on the floor and all the contents scattered about. The other windows still had their curtains closed, preventing me from seeing in. I swung the telescope down to view the back of the house again, seeing nothing more than before. Suddenly a form strode into view from the kitchen area—a werewolf Priest. It was snarling at something I couldn't see. Suddenly it burst out of the house and into the yard, looked around, then dashed to the side of the house.

Suddenly the rear door burst open and what looked like a human came running out. It was Maisie.

Her dress was torn, she was obviously preggers, and there was blood on her face and dress. She stumbled and fell to her knees. The door burst open again, and a group of werewolves ran out heading towards her, followed by the Priest. The pack surrounded Maisie and began slashing at her with their hands, and snapping with their teeth, in what seemed like an effort to herd her back inside.

The Priest ran up and began kicking her in the stomach. Maisie screamed, clutched at her stomach, and started to writhe. This went on for what seemed like an eternity. The Priest jumped on Maisie and tore at her stomach with his mouth and hands. Reaching down, he grabbed on to something, and jumped back with it.

Oh, Christ.

It was a baby. Maisie's baby, ripped from her womb. Maisie was screaming. The pack of Drones stopped their slashing and jumped on her.

I sat bolt upright with shock and indecision. There was nothing I could do to help my friend. I rocked back and forth for the space of few heartbeats. A sudden, chilling decision froze my movements.

Standing quickly, I took out the hunting rifle from the

nearby case, slapped in a magazine, and worked the bolt to put a round into the firing chamber. Turning back towards the window, I rested the barrel of the rifle on the windowsill, and removed the caps from the sighting scope. The sighting scope didn't have anywhere near the power of the telescope, of course. The group of werewolves attacking Maisie looked like some writhing nightmare creature.

I fired one shot after another, quickly working the bolt to put round after round into the firing chamber. I aimed towards the centre of the group, bracketing the shots. Eventually the hammer clicked on an empty chamber when I pulled the trigger. My breathing started becoming ragged. I forced myself to calmness as I pulled the rifle back and laid it across the table.

Returning to the telescope, I adjusted it to focus on the Frontenac house. I felt cold as ice, both physically and mentally, as I surveyed the area. The werewolves were glancing about trying to locate the source of the gunshots. They stood there for a few moments before dashing into the house. No-one human went with them.

I adjusted the telescope slightly to examine what remained. There were several bodies—at least three, and possibly more. I stared at the bodies for some time before concluding that nothing on the ground was ever going to move again. A flash of movement caught my eye, and I adjusted the telescope to look at the windows. Brief shadows could be seen flitting across the drawn curtains.

I calmly took a full magazine and replaced the empty one. Repositioning the rifle, I fired into the windows whenever a shadow appeared, until the hammer clicked on an empty chamber.

After that I felt nothing. Not numb, not empty... just nothing. I sat there staring out the window, blinking. It all looked so peaceful as I stared out. It was only when viewed under magnification that the horror became evident. I inhaled sharply as another set of thoughts struck me. What about my other neighbours? What about the Town and beyond? Maybe I'd been living in the eye of the hurricane for weeks and never knew it. With phone lines dead and the roads too dangerous to travel, what else might be happening that I wasn't able to find out about?

The next question was, what to do about it? What could one old man do against that tsunami of horror engulfing the area? Where were the police?

I forced myself to take slow, careful breaths. Events were moving too rapidly for me to process. There had to be a pattern, something to give everything meaning. The non-feeling state was beginning to shatter as my thoughts raced. Despite my best efforts, my face twisted into a snarl and my breathing became ragged and gasping. The world began to shake and whirl around me, as I fell to my knees. My arms hung limply. My hands crumpled on the floor beside me.

A great weariness engulfed me, and I almost succumbed to it. How could I possibly survive? What was the point of going on or even trying?

The bleakness almost won.

Yet a fire still raged inside me that would not be extinguished by anything other than death. Yes, I was in the middle of what seemed to be the arrival of Hell on Earth. Yes, I was just one tired old man. But fuck that shit, and fuck the werewolves.

I had spent my life being ignored and kicked about and taken advantage of—and having to just take it for the sake of earning a paycheque. Then came my chance in retirement to make a place for myself and live the way I wanted to. To make a place that I could truly call a home and find some peace away from all the crap in the world.

Most of my neighbours were good people. The few assholes could easily be ignored. It was a great life. Without warning, it all went bad because Something wanted to smash it, just like it had all gone wrong for me in the past. Before the farm, economic necessity required me to bow my head and either take the shit or try to evade it, with fighting back never an option.

Not this time.

Never again.

This was my home. This was my last, best chance at making a life for myself that I could be happy with. Now, Something wanted me to surrender, to bend to its will, to give up everything again.

Fuck that shit, now and forever.

My bowed head slowly rose up. I took a couple of deep, calming breaths, and began the effort to stand up. First the right leg moved until the foot was flat on the floor. My right hand went onto the knee. I levered myself up until I was standing upright. The slight swaying was gone within a couple of breaths. I was focused and ready to face the world.

The first task was to gather information. Time to break out the UAV—unmanned aerial vehicle. The local OPP hated those things, and gave me hell even when I used them only on my own property. I had stashed them away for an emergency, and this certainly qualified. There were two of them, one small cheapie that had about a kilometre range max before its batteries ran out. The big one was gas-powered and had three times the range and could carry a half-kilo payload in addition to its camera. Both of them could transmit decent-quality video for their entire range.

I went back to the ground floor and dug out the cheapie. After making sure that it was charged up, I gave it a brief indoor test, and it all checked out. Ensuring that everything was safe outside, I opened the side door, took the UAV out, and placed it about three metres away. After turning on the power, I hurried back inside. Grabbing the control unit and VR goggles, I went back to the sniper nest and sat down. I gave the motors some juice, lifted off, and headed out at about ten metres above the ground. The little thing made an angry buzz as it flew away.

The modest range of the device made the choice of target the Jackson farm about half a kilometre away. I'd forgotten how much fun these were to fly, and was beginning to enjoy the experience when the house came into view. Ignoring the rear of the house, which I could see it from the sniper nest anyway, I sent the drone to the front of the house.

That showed a different story, but no longer a shocking one.

There were several smeared trails of what I assumed to be blood. They led from various points in the driveway and near the house, and converged towards the barn. The barn held their modest herd of dairy cows. Seeing that one of the barn doors was open, I flew the UAV towards it and hovered just outside. The inside was lit only by the daylight shining in, which made it dim but viewable by the UAV's camera. After seeing nothing of interest from the outside, I carefully entered the barn. I slowly spun the UAV about its axis to get a complete view of the inside, and rather wished that I hadn't. The scene resembled the inside of a slaughter house. There were dismembered remains scattered into numerous small piles, and blood was everywhere. Some of the remains were obviously bovine, although the smaller ribcage coming into view looked far too human.

I let the UAV hover there for a few seconds while I recovered my equilibrium, then spun it around and began navigating out. A sudden movement caught my attention, and I cut speed to hover. A mistake—it spun madly and fell to the floor. It landed with the camera facing upward, and I could see the savage face of a Priest coming towards the UAV. In its hand was a stick obviously being used as a club. The crude club arced down towards the camera lens and everything went black. The status lights in the VR goggles showed that the signal had been lost.

It appeared that the werewolves had overtaken the local farms. Equally disturbing, if that was the correct term, was that they now seemed to be using weapons. An unforeseen and horrible development. All the other Changed had lost their interest in tools of any sort, reverting to a simple, bestial animal nature. It was becoming obvious that the Priests were a whole new class of Changed. They organized, they planned, they learnt, they used tools, and they were tremendously aggressive.

Where were the authorities?

The phone lines had been dead for weeks, but no-one had been out to fix things that I could tell. Hell, where were the damn cops? How far did the Priest's eradication campaign extend? Why was Maisie kept alive—until today, anyway? I needed more information, and quickly.

The big UAV seemed like the only way to go about getting it, so I began prepping it for use. That should have taken me ten minutes, fifteen at the outside. My hands were clumsy and prone to shaking so badly that it took me nearly thirty-five minutes to finish the task. After a check of the security system showed that everything was clear, I took the machine outside, placed it on the ground, and went back inside to the sniper nest.

Both UAVs were controlled from the same VR headset and controller, which made things easier. I signalled the motors to start, and they all revved quickly. After a check to make sure that the camera worked fine, I steered the UAV up and out. This time I headed for the road, planning to follow it towards the nearest town to see what I could find.

The UAV had gone about a kilometre down the road, further than I had managed to drive for quite some time, when I spotted a utility van that had apparently careened into the ditch. I approached, being careful to keep the drone four or five metres off the ground. Circling the van, which was from the local telephone repair depot, I could see a number of bloody trails that led off to a large jumble of remains. The van had not veered; it had hit a line of Drones who appeared to have been used as a barrier. That would explain the lack of traffic.

Maybe I should have investigated sooner. Traffic was normally sparse on my stretch of road, but I should have suspected something. Tamping down the self-recriminations that I didn't have time for, I continued down the road, scanning left and right. I detected a flash of movement just outside the copse of trees on the left, and I slowed to get a better look. It looked like the tail end of a column of people—or werewolves. As I carefully moved towards the trees, I made sure that I was out of reach of anything leaping upwards and hard to hit by any thrown object. I hoped.

Just inside the line of trees I could see human-looking shapes. Suddenly, one of them jumped up and started waving—it looked like a regular human woman! Several other women jumped up and started waving until they were dragged down and forced deeper into the brush with blows to their heads and bodies. The copse was a large one, and there was no possibility of tracking the group within it. After a moment's hesitation, I reluctantly decided to keep flying down the road. The fuel level was a bit above half full—that is, I would soon hit the point of no return.

There was another grouping of trees up ahead, which I decided to make my next target of investigation. By this point I was just past the turnoff to the side-road that led to the Frontenac house. At the point where the road curved around the dense trees to either side, I swerved the UAV around them and suddenly saw the crashed remains of a police cruiser. Like the telephone repair van, it appeared that Drones had been used as a living barrier.

Movement up ahead caught my eye and I gunned the engines to go ahead as quickly as possible. It was another line of people walking, and they were far enough from the trees that I should be able to get a good look if I hurried.

As before, the group was a mixture of werewolves and humans—women, in various states of dress. The werewolves looked up and snarled at the UAV as they drove the women into the trees as quickly as they could run. I got a clear look at them before they vanished into the woods. The werewolves were all Priests. The women ranged in age, ranging from teenagers to middle aged-ish. All looked to be in decent physical condition, if a bit tattered and dirty.

The control system told me that the UAV was low on fuel. I had reached the cut-off point, and had to fly it back or lose it. With a heavy heart, I turned the machine back home. My mind was in something of a turmoil. On the one hand, I desperately wanted to help the women held captive by the Priests. On the other hand, there was nothing I could do. Nothing at all.

On yet another hand, I had important new information about new behaviour by the Priests. Where were they taking the women? And why?

I stopped thinking about all that, and focused on getting the UAV back home safely. It managed to get near to the barn, and about two metres above the ground, when the fuel ran out. It fell heavily to the ground. I ripped the VR headset from my head and dashed outside to retrieve the machine without even checking the security system. I grabbed the UAV, hauled it into the barn, and made sure that the door was bolted.

The werewolves, led by the Priests, were purging the area of humans, except for women within a certain age range. Wait a minute—those were women of breeding age. Were they being rounded up for breeding stock, or something worse? The movement I saw was probably the process of transporting the women to some central location. Being driven like cattle.

This was beyond a disease issue. This was beyond war. This was a program of extermination.

I was probably the last human in the area. My killing of their nest in the Frontenac house, and buzzing around with the UAVs, had no doubt turned their attentions back towards me. That, combined with the probe-in-force earlier today, meant that they were probably going to try to finish me off Real Soon Now. Which behove me to beef up my defences right away.

The first thing to do was to set out the various spike barriers. Those were new, and they wouldn't be expecting those. The two remaining mortars were already loaded, as were all the cannons. I still had a feeling that I needed something new. OK, I'd let that percolate while I set out the spike barriers, and I set about doing just that. It took less than half an hour to finish, and it all looked so much more pathetic than I had hoped.

In an attempt to improve things, I attached some more spikes, including some of the special caltrops, around various areas like the greenhouse and the generator cages. That cheered me up some.

There was one last weapon to set out—a sort of doomsday device that could hurt me as much as the werewolves. I had a decent quantity of various caustic liquids in the form of toilet cleaners and such. Within an hour I had filled up a large quantity of fragile containers—glass jars, old incandescent light bulbs, and the like—with various nasty liquids. The ugly thing about them was not just their immediate effects, but also the toxic gases produced when they combined. These containers could be broken by being stepped on or by one of my explosive devices. The randomness of that appealed to me.

It was getting dark by the time I finished. After making one last hurried check around the barn to make sure that everything was secure, I headed back to the house. Things were as ready as I could make them, and I wanted to take the opportunity to wash up and eat some food. It had been a long day.

The attack came later that night.

CHAPTER THIRTEEN
Reaching Out To Friends

TO : all
FROM : Felix
SUBJECT : All the shit has hit the fan

Summary : All Hell has broken loose. My position here is no longer defensible. I plan to leave here within 2 days, at the latest.

Hey, Gang :

Things are bad and about to get worse. The shitstorm that has hit the countryside is bound to get to the cities sooner than later.

There was a big attack last night—I figure the previous one was just a feint to probe my defences. Think about that for a minute.

I'm fine, the house and barn are unbreached, but the greenhouse, gardens, outside power generators, and windmills are trashed beyond any reasonable hope of repair. There are dead werewolves covering my yard, but

I'm not going to bother cleaning them up. I'll go out later and take some high-res pics of them and hopefully that will be of some use. I'll also send out some pics of the attack. If the bandwidth allows, I'll include some videos. It is important that you learn about this right away.

The New Werewolves are worse than we thought. They are smart and aggressive. They are organizers and tool-users. They can forge all the other types of werewolves into a cooperative group. They are also systematically killing every human in the area, with the exception of women of child-bearing age. They are using any buildings they find as shelters. That's where they seem to be keeping the captured women, but that's a tentative conclusion based on limited data. It also appears that troublesome women are disciplined into submission or killed.

The organization of the werewolves doesn't appear to be pack-based any more, but rather a larger type of social unit. I've yet to see any evidence of infighting or fighting between groups led by the New Werewolves, which I call Priests. (Those are the ones with the strange bodies and markings on them). In fact, all I've seen and experienced is massive cooperation. In each battle that they've taken part in, the Priests are adept at organizing and wielding masses of the Old Type Werewolves (which I call Drones). The latter seem be willing to do whatever they are told. That implies a hierarchy, with the Priests at the top and the Drones at the bottom to varying degrees.

Remember what Lee said about the plague growth curves found on those old artifacts? They showed one more Change Plague than we've experienced. Given what I've seen, I suspect that the next Plague is to create the ruling class. Or perhaps an improved version of the Priests. That would be very bad. What we seem to have here is a new species. One that is becoming organized with one goal—to eliminate humans. To what end, I cannot say, though I think that conclusion is inescapable.

As for my own condition, I'm tired but unhurt. The power lines are dead. The solar panels are sufficient to maintain the computer systems and food freezers indefinitely. Of more immediate concern is the destruction of the greenhouse and gardens. I can probably salvage a lot of the root vegetables, and that's about it. The Priests appear to have led the attack on the greenhouse to get rid of the garlic and wolfsbane, and then the others were brought in to finish the job.

That means that the passive defences that everyone has depended are no longer effective, since the Priests don't seem to be allergic to the usual plants. The only thing that saved my ass was that the werewolves don't seem to use fire at all. Repelling the attack forced me to use up the bulk of my consumable munitions, whether bullets or gas or fluids. Sheer brute force, wielding clubs, will eventually allow them to break into the house and barn.

So, it is time for me to get the hell out of Dodge. I can fill the truck up with foodstuffs and essential tech. I've got enough gas left to fill it up and then some. I've got a snow plow that I can affix to the front, and that'll let me smash through almost anything after I beef up the supports. I'll set up the house and barn for full automatic operation, including defences.

This redoubt was always meant as an insurance policy for us. Now it'll just have to act as a bank, securing all the food and books and tech until we can come back to reclaim it. I'll rig traps and such inside the house, and will be sure to send you details on how to bypass and disarm it all, before I leave. I'll also post warning signs to warn off any humans that might have survived. Doubt there are any, but I'll do it anyways. It'll take me a least a day, possibly more, to set all this up so that's my timeline.

Without exaggeration, Hell is coming. After beating back this last attack, I think I've put the fear of Humans into this lot, for a time. The only way to beat back any new attack is with poison gas, and I've few stocks to generate much of that. I may have a one or two other options, but nothing that'll buy me much more time.

I'll come down with copies of all my data, of course. If there are some specific hard copies of stuff any of you might specifically want, let me know ASAP. Keep in mind that my limited cargo space, please!

One last point, and this is important and no-fooling-around serious. You need to let me know if you've got space for me. You've got to give this a serious think before answering. Most of what I could offer has to be left behind. If you say "no", I've got alternate routes and plans—you have my word of honour on that. Think about it and let me know.

Felix

CHAPTER FOURTEEN
Abandon Ship

I felt better after sending the last email. The die was cast, and the path was clear. Despite my bone-deep weariness and the fuzziness welling up inside my mind, I couldn't afford to rest just yet. I paused to sip some water and nibble a piece of bread as I tried to decide what needed doing first. Swivelling back and forth slightly, I let my gaze flick across the main consoles as I rocked. It was difficult to work up the energy to move, but a list of tasks began to assemble itself in my mind.

One step in front of the other. March or die.

I took a look to confirm that there were no threats detected. It all seemed OK, even though some of the IR detectors and cameras were non-functional.

The first task was to replace all the point defence shotgun shells in the house. I heaved myself up to my feet and headed to the main storage area in the basement. I grabbed a couple boxes of shotgun shells and a box of replacement wall inserts, then headed upstairs. My stocks of both were almost gone, but there was enough to reload everything.

The task of replacing the shotgun shells and wall inserts along the walls at each point defence cell was a pleasantly simple task. All but one of the cells had been triggered during the final wave. Some of the inserts that I pulled out had blood on them. I ignored the mess and just tossed them to one side. Cleaning up was not on my list of things to do any more. I wasn't quite sure how I felt about that.

Next on the list was repeating the same process in the barn. The armoury in the barn should have enough shells and wall inserts remaining, so all I took with me was a camera. And the obligatory shotgun, just in case.

I stepped carefully while walking. The reason for my concern was not for another attack, but avoiding the corpses and puddles of icky stuff. Paranoia also made me worry about not-entirely-dead werewolves. I used a remote temperature sensor to check each body as I walked by it. Everything was showing as the same temperature as the ground, which was what I was expecting. It was tempting to not waste time checking, but the habits ingrained over the past few years kept that feeling in check. Barely.

As I went along, I made sure to take plenty of pictures of the more intact corpses. There were lots to choose from, and some weren't in bad shape. I suppose it depended on which wave they were in, to some extent. There were a few Priest corpses here, though none that would be useful for a photograph. Interestingly, some of the Drones had symbols carved into their faces similar to ones worn by the Priests. That was new, so photographs of those were in order.

So much carnage. So much death. I suppose I should have felt something. The tsunami of events over the past few days had just left me numb.

Eventually I got to the side door of the barn, and let myself in. To prove to myself that I was functioning at a high level, I told the security console to run a full scan. I figured it would be a good idea to check inside and out of the building that I'd had to defend remotely.

Everything was fine except for the blockage of a few of the ground level scanners at the rear of the barn. Using the video feeds I could see that the problem was caused by corpses that had fallen forward so as to block them. The IR sensors indicated that the bodies were as cold as the ground, so they could be ignored for now.

It appeared that all the point defence cells were blown and needed replacing. I grabbed a couple of boxes of shotgun shells and wall inserts from the armoury, and began the process.

Again, it was a straightforward task that helped me maintain and strengthen my mental equilibrium.

With the ground floor done, I went upstairs to replace a few upper level cells that had been blown. That rather intrigued me, I must admit, since there were no trees nearby. Perhaps they had tried to get into an upper window by standing on each other's shoulders, or maybe something totally unexpected. In any case, the attempt had killed them. For the moment it was sufficient to replace the expended cells.

After finishing with that, I went into the sniper nest and used the binoculars to take a thorough look around. The destruction of the greenhouse and gardens caused my eyes to tear up, and I had to pause to compose myself and wipe my eyes. I even had to blow my nose a few times. Those things had represented a hope for the future, a way to provide for myself and my friends. Now it was all in ruins.

The two windmills were trashed. One was lying on the ground, with a couple of corpses crushed beneath it. The other was missing its blades. Judging by the stains on the housing, the Drones had simply thrust their hands into the blades to grab hold of them. The first few attempts would have lopped off or crushed limbs. After that, the blades would have slowed down or jammed, allowing the remaining Drones to finish the job.

The propane generator was smashed, even though it had been enclosed inside a solid cage. Obviously not solid enough. There was no evidence of any leaks around the large propane tank, so it appeared the shutoff valves all worked like they were designed to. I would have to do something about that tank at some point. Maybe drain it. Otherwise it was a bomb waiting to happen.

There were a few bodies there, including some Priests. Those would be worth photographing in detail, if only to gauge the effect of the garlic and wolfsbane on them compared to the Drones. I noted that most of the Drones had been badly affected, but the Priests not so much. I scanned around my property, paying particular attention to anything that looked like a Drone with markings.

During the attack, some of the Drones seemed to be in

charge of groups of other Drones. More new behaviour. I'd have to check the videos carefully, but my gut feeling was that the Drones with special markings seemed to have been in some sort of leadership role.

The one bright spot was that the solar panels looked fine, and were generating at full power.

Putting down the binoculars, I made a series of panoramic pictures with the camera, take care to overlap each shot with the next. I'd do another series of the front yard that was obscured by the house from this location. As feared, the Priests had taken care of the caltrops I'd spread around by simply driving Drones through them. The lengths of lumber with nails had been dealt with in a similar fashion.

On the plus side, the Drones used to clear away the spikes with their bodies had become maddened with pain. Their panic had caused all sorts of confusion and fear amongst the rest of the werewolves as they ran away from the battle. One of the few mistakes made by the Priests, and it had given me a breathing space to prepare the next layers of defence.

At that point I had turned on the sonic generators. That caused more of the Drones to panic and leave the battleground. It also seemed to make it more difficult for the Priests and their sub-commanders to issue orders. That added to the confusion and less-than-perfect coordination of attacks. The wide garden beds of garlic and wolfsbane had protected the front of the house surprisingly well, and the bulk of the attackers carried on toward the rear. Any of them who got close to the front wall got taken out by the point defence cells, and that effectively ended the attack there.

Unfortunately, the main target of the attack had been the greenhouse and gardens. The other waves of attacks were not feints, as such, just led by Drone sub-commanders instead of Priests. The Priests hit the gardens surrounding the greenhouse and tore out the garlic and wolfsbane plants. Then they smashed into the greenhouse using their clubs, and disposed of the garlic and wolfsbane inside it. That left the way clear for the Drones to come in and finish the job. Something which they appeared to do with great relish.

I had been distracted by the simultaneous attacks on several fronts, and had let loose with noxious fluids (artificial skunk spray and high-strength vinegar). That drove them away from the house itself, allowing me to fire the remaining two mortars into their midst. The blasts had damaged the house walls somewhat, but had shredded the werewolves. I had managed to shoot many of the retreaters from the attic.

The ones who had attacked the barn got hit by air cannons firing grapeshot. It was amazing how effective a pair of ball bearings with a length of piano wire between them can be in slicing through flesh. Short lengths of chain did a serviceable job at that task, too. In any event, the massed charges got broken up quite nicely. The sonic generators disoriented the survivors, and broke any semblance of control that the Priests might have had.

The battle had ended with me being victorious, though at a terribly high cost. I'd lost much of my garden crop for the year, and depleted the bulk of my ammunition. In all probability this victory had only bought me a few days of peace, if that.

I brought myself up to full alert with a start. I'd been replaying the events of the previous night over in my head, and I couldn't afford the time for that right now. Taking a deep breath, I exhaled slowly in an attempt to force myself into a focused state. There was too much to do, and little time to do it in.

Returning to the main floor, I decided to use the opportunity to fill the gas tank of the truck. It was a large industrial pickup with a crew cab, and a bed large enough to hold a sheet of plywood. A brute of machine with enough power for practically any task.

After topping up its gas, I pondered if I should put on the snow plow now or later. I decided to do it later, after taking pictures of any of the Priests around the ruined greenhouse. The Group needed the information more than they needed me, quite frankly.

Suddenly I felt incredibly tired, and had to lean my head against the coolness of the truck's body. I felt tears coming to my eyes and running down my cheeks. I angrily brushed them away, but they kept leaking out, and soon sobs accompanied them.

The analytical part of my mind sat back and analyzed this as an emotional reaction to the battle. Another part of me felt old and sad that I'd reached the point in my life where my life was no longer worth much to anyone. Yet another part of me began working through mindfulness exercises, focusing on the situation without judging.

Gradually my tears stopped and my sobs reduced to mild gasps. I focused on keeping my breathing, and my thoughts, slow and even. Self-control slowly returned. Wiping my eyes on my sleeves, I went over to the closest sink and washed my face with cold water. I dried it with a paper towel, which I threw on the floor.

I forced myself to look around and analyze the situation. Taking a deep breath, I decided that although the time was not right to attach the plow, it couldn't hurt to locate it. I used to know where everything was, but my mind was in too much of a jumble to focus clearly.

After looking around, I saw it at the back hanging from the wall. It was a big V-plow, and not something I'd be moving easily. It would take the tractor to lift it off the wall and bring it to the truck for attachment. OK, so that meant that it was a task for later—probably just before I was ready to go. Yes, it made sense to load up first, before attaching any external devices. Taking another deep breath, I decided to take advantage of the daylight and carry on with the initial task of taking pictures.

With that, I exited the garage area and went outside. The door bolts slammed home behind me. I realized that I'd forgotten to check the security console to see if there were any threats detected. Piss on it, I decided, and headed towards the ruined greenhouse. At least I had remembered to bring the IR thermometer with me to check the bodies. I took photographs of all the Priest bodies I could find, even going so far as to roll them over to photograph them from all angles. I'd not seen intact ones up close before, and was fascinated despite myself.

They were stocky brutes, with a distinct muzzle. Pushing back the gums, I could see that the teeth seemed to be carnivore teeth, with no molars. They were covered in mud, with symbols of some sort carved into the mud. All had a single symbol carved into the flesh of the left cheek. I took quite a few close-up pictures of the faces, hands, and feet. As Gail had suspected, their knee joints looked strange. Not quite bent backwards like a dog's, but very creepy. Might explain the strange loping run that I'd noticed during the attack.

Most of the Drones had markings that matched the symbols on the Priests carved into their arms and cheeks. It occurred to me to wonder how such scarification was done without medical problems occurring. That, however, was a question for another time and place. Right now, I needed to focus on gathering data and sending it out.

After photographing anything that looked useful, I went back into the house. I stored my gear then headed downstairs. A wave of weakness forced me to stop. I'd been pushing myself too hard on too little sleep.

Concentrating for a few moments on controlling my breathing, I stood upright, and walked back into the kitchen. I put the camera on the table, then went to the sink and forced myself to drink a large glass of water. It was time to take care of myself first, before I collapsed. So I went upstairs to have a shower and change my clothes. Maybe have a nap.

The world might be ending but I was determined to meet it clean and fresh, if not bright-eyed and bushy-tailed.

★ ★ ★

The shower perked me up enough that I decided to forgo the nap, and focus on getting some work done. The first step was to get some food. A hearty sandwich and some coffee would be just the thing. With a couple cups of coffee in me, I would be assured that any nap I took would be brief. The filling of my bladder would see to that, if nothing else.

I slung the camera, grabbed the sandwich and coffee, and headed to the basement. Once there, I took a big bite from the sandwich, chewed it with gusto, and washed it down with a big swig of coffee. After nourishing the inner man, I took the memory card out of the camera and began the process of decanting the pictures to the main computer. After a moment's thought, I decided that now was as good a time as any to copy the videos taken by the UAVs from the barn's computer to the main one in preparation for making copies of everything.

With that task started, I grabbed some more bites from the sandwich before I swung over to the communications displays. The satellite link was up and working at full bandwidth for a change. There were several dozen messages, most of them spam. The spam I deleted without even looking at them, and repeated that process for the ones from my distant family members. I had no time to waste on them right now. That left me with a half a dozen or so messages from The Group. Those were important.

Looking at them in order from oldest to newest, there were a couple from Dixon and Grant expressing worry about my safety after the last attack. Each said to stop being such a moron and head down ASAP. The next one was from Stan. He said that they'd had a mini-conference about it, and there were two solid places for me to stay—Lee's apartment or his house. It was my decision, but he was worried about Lee and Gail being on their own. Her apartment was in an older low-rise in a decent area, but it wasn't as defensible as his house by any stretch of the imagination. Of all The Group, they were the least able to withstand a siege. On a side note, none of his sources had mentioned anything about attacks outside of the city. He ended by telling me to stay safe, and get my ass to Toronto ASAP.

The next one was from Lee, and she assured me that I would be more than welcome to stay with her. It was gratifying to hear that, 'cuz I knew she wouldn't bullshit me. We'd worked together years ago, and had stayed friends despite the difference in our ages. She was a talented woman, but not the best of cooks, so that was something that I could help her with.

The last email was from Gail, asking me to bring back some sample bodies of the werewolves. The request set me back in the chair with a start, and I read the sentence again. I gave my head a shake, and scrubbed my face with my hands.

Ick. Ick and yuck and no way, Jose.

With an angry snort I leaned forward to read the rest of her email. It said to stop being squeamish and think, dammit.

Harrumph—it was like she could see me.

It turns out that there were no verifiable reports of the Priest-type werewolf anywhere. It was deadly important to get one for a full autopsy. It would also be REALLY NICE (her emphasis) to get a sample of the latest types of Drones. That is, the non-Priest ones marked with symbols. And, if I had room, one of the regular Drones. She emphasized how important this was and, oh, how excited she was that I was safe and going to be staying with them.

Harrumph, again.

I sat there for a minute with my hand cradling my mouth—the Jack Benny pose, as my late father used to call it. What the hell did they think I was, a hearse service? I had never actually touched a corpse before, and those things had been sitting outside for nearly a day. No, no, it couldn't be done.

Yet even as I sat there shaking my head at the impossibility of it all, the analytical part of my mind was busily sorting through the logic tree and tossing out ways and means of doing it.

Shit. It could be done. In theory. I guess.

My cogitating (a much kinder term than "wool gathering") was interrupted by an alert indicating another email had come in. This one was from Lee, but signed from both her and Gail. They told me to head straight to the ROM loading docks when I came down, so as to decant the specimens as quickly as possible to the lab. The cell towers were still working, mostly, along Highway 400 south of Highway 9, so be sure to give them a call when I got that far. Oh, and drive safely.

Well, shit. Looked like I wasn't going to be given a choice here. I made an amused snort. The girls were right—this was new information and we needed all of that we could get. On the other hand, the videos and pics were important as well.

Alrighty then, new plan—bug out ASAP.

Interesting that the cell phones were working south of Highway 9, though. That was roughly the halfway point between here and Toronto. It was also the dividing line between the Greater Toronto Area and the rural areas. Did that have any significance in light of the attacks?

Giving my head a shake, I forced myself to focus on the immediate tasks. There were specimens to gather up and prepare for transport. There was data to be collected, and copies made for transport. Supplies to be gathered. The house and barn needed to be prepped for an indefinite absence. My computers needed to be set up for remote access, so The Group could download the data. Just in case something happened to me along the way.

Oh, and I needed to get a few hours of rest before leaving. It was going to be a long trip, with city driving at the end.

Damn, but I hated driving in Toronto. The thought of driving downtown to the ROM with my truck frightened me, I'm not ashamed to say. Would have preferred to beat off attacks by werewolves, almost. That thought, initially amusing, sobered up my thinking right quick. This wasn't a simple day trip. This was abandoning my home. My life.

Suddenly my eyes began leaking, and I had to wipe them and blow my nose. There was so much here. So much I wanted to save. Leaving it all behind for an uncertain future as refugee was a crushing prospect. I dried my eyes one last time and gave my nose a final blow. This was war—a war of survival unlike anything the world had ever seen. The feelings of one useless pathetic old man didn't matter. I had a job to do and I needed to get on with it.

The first task, gathering specimens, was fully as distasteful as I had expected it to be. After pondering the technical details for a bit, I came up with an appropriate technique. The first step was to lay down a tarp of heavy plastic. After that, I levered the body onto the tarp with a shovel, and rolled body plus tarp into a tube shape. The open ends got folded onto the body of the tube, and sealed with duct tape. Over that went a pair of heavy-duty plastic yard waste bags, sealed with more duct tape. There was a final layer of plastic tarp, again sealed with duct tape. That ought to keep the ooky stuff and smell contained, I figured.

I blessed duct tape as being only second to fire as a gift from the gods.

An hour later, I had three specimens all packaged up, plus

another package of bits and pieces—a few extra heads of each type, plus some limbs from as many different bodies as I could stuff in. I figured that might be useful for building up a DNA database.

After reflection, I made up another package of just Priest bits. They were something new, so the more details we could gather on them the better. Completing that, I went back to the barn and used the tractor to transport the bodies to the garage. For the time being, I dumped them in a line from front to back of the garage so they wouldn't interfere with getting anything out. That would keep them out of the sun, and the unheated concrete floor would help to keep them cool. Keeping the specimens cool was a Good Thing, as far as I was concerned.

OK, the specimens were gathered and readied for transport. What to do next? Was there anything in the barn or garage that I needed right now? I took a quick look around but couldn't think of anything. The truck was all gassed up and ready to go, requiring only loading up. The attachment of the V-plow would get done just before I left.

It occurred to me that I'd need to clear a path to the road, and right now the driveway was littered with bodies and caltrops. Backing the tractor out of the garage, I lowered the scoop and made several passes to clear the driveway out as far as the road. The bodies I simply dumped to the side of the driveway as I went. Let 'em serve as a warning to the others, I figured. Or maybe a meal. Whatever.

As I headed back to the barn, I could see that I'd not gotten all the caltrops off the driveway. Damn. Although the tractor's tires were thick enough to absorb the spikes without being punctured, the truck's tires were not. Well, that was going to be a problem, since even one punctured tires would put an ignominious end to my escape. Back at the barn, I went to the machine shop area and grabbed a couple of the magnetic brooms used to pick up anything ferrous off the floor. I used some duct tape and cable ties to attach them to the front of the scoop.

Another idea occurred to me, and I wrapped a two-metre length of 4x4 beam with thick foam and attached that to the rear of the tractor with chains. With the gear in place, I went back over the driveway. The magnetic brooms attracted, and the dragged beam impaled, the caltrops. I had to stop a couple of times to slide all the collected caltrops off the magnets, and it all seemed to be working well. When I finished, I took off the used foam, re-wrapped with new foam, then repeated the process. There were no more caltrops embedded in the foam, so it appeared that I'd gotten them all. If not, this would be a very short trip.

I made a note to attach the magnetic brooms to the front of the V-plow before I left, just to play it safe. The idea of playing it safe given the situation got me chuckling for a moment. My weariness didn't allow that to last too long, though. Locking up the barn, I headed back to the house. It was time to grab a bite to eat and gather up supplies.

After entering the kitchen I decided to have a decent meal, rather than something gulped down. I really needed a chance to sit and gather my thoughts. I'd had the fact that I wasn't a young man any more hammered into me repeatedly over the past little while, so I decided to take the hint. Besides, it was beginning to get dark and my body clock said that it was supper time.

I made up a hearty stir-fry and forced myself to eat it relatively slowly, using the time to make a list of what I needed to take with me. The bodies of the werewolves were really going to eat into the available space in the truck. After a moment's thought, I realized that I could offset that by packing frozen foods around the bodies, and placing the fluffy stuff like clothing on top of that.

Multitasking the packing would certainly help make best use of the space. I was beginning to think of the bodies as just another item to carry. I suppose one can get used to darn near anything, given time.

That would take care of some of the food. Stuff like flour and beans and rice and seasonings, I was already storing in one- and five-gallon containers. Easy enough just to toss them in. Not as many as I would have liked, but enough to be useful. Weapons were another issue, though. For one thing, I had too many to transport all at once. More importantly, cops frowned on heavily-armed civilians driving around. Although rural cops usually allowed a shotgun for protection, Toronto cops still had a zero-tolerance policy. Except for themselves and the Important People, of course.

Well, I could hide some of the weapons and ammunition amongst the food and bedding in the back easily enough. I'd certainly wear my revolver and have a couple of the shotguns with me in the cab. They could be hidden when I got closer to the city.

As for the data I had on hand, that raised other issues. The printouts I could put into backpacks and such. As for personal effects, several changes in clothes and toiletry supplies could be tossed into a knapsack or duffel bag or something. Add a sleeping bag and some blankets, and that would do me, I guess. Oh, and a laptop or two and some paper and pens. Damn, it was all adding up very damn fast. The truck was going to be full, both in the bed and the cab. I needed to keep the load down enough to have a clear line of sight through all the windows, which was going to put a severe limit on how much I could take.

The thought of leaving all my books behind was like a physical blow. I'd been a bibliophile all my life, and cherished each and every book I had. On top of that, I'd become The Group's keeper of the dead tree material, as I had more library space than the rest of them combined. Taking a deep calming breath I told myself that I'd be coming back one of these days, either to re-settle here or do a proper salvage job. That helped some, but it still hurt to think about what I was leaving behind.

Which reminded me to include some of my toolkits in the list of things to take. I definitely would need tools of various sorts. Those were all in containers, so it would be easy to grab what was needed. The ache of having to leave some of those behind was as great as the thought of leaving the books behind. I've always thought that fine tools were a joy to use, or even just hold in the hands.

Shaking my head, I forced myself to focus on the task that I was trying to avoid thinking about. OK, the kitchen could be used as a staging area for a lot of this stuff to get it set up for transport to the truck. Quick snacks and a thermos of coffee and water got added to the list of things to put in the cab. With a sigh I got to my feet and carried my dirty dishes to the sink. With an amused grunt I just put them off to one side of the counter. No need to wash up anything here, not any more.

With that cheery thought in mind I made a quick plan for staging supplies in the limited kitchen space to maximize the efficiency of loading everything later. I decided to begin by stacking containers of dry food to one side over there, and ammunitions and weapons over there, and tools and books over there, and stuff for the cab towards the rear. Yeah, that sounded about right. I had work to do and a plan to get it done. What more could a man ask for?

After hauling up food, weapons, and knapsacks of the printouts and reports I had generated, I decided to have a small snack, then get a bit of sleep. The actual loading up could wait until I had rested.

With that, I headed upstairs and lay back on my bed. Possibly for the last time. I was damn tired, but still wound up. After a few minutes of failing to get to sleep, I jerked upright and set the clock alarm to wake me up about an hour before dawn. Finishing up the packing should take an hour or so, and I still needed to set the house and barn systems to full standby. Best to start before too much of the morning went by. There were so many things to do, that I started listing them out in my head.

It wasn't too long after that that I dropped off.

CHAPTER FIFTEEN
The Great Escape

I actually woke up about an hour before the alarm was set to go off. After a quick wash-up I was ready to start the day. It was going to be a long and busy one.

Heading down to the kitchen, I made a sketchy breakfast. Putting the dirty dishes aside, I put the coffee on to brew, set some water to boiling, and grabbed several thermos bottles from the pantry. One for the coffee, one for hot water, one for cold water, and the other for whatever. Maybe heat up some soup or stew and toss it into the thermos bottle—yeah, that sounded like a fine idea. If it didn't get eaten along the way, the girls would enjoy it. Thinking of them, I grabbed one of the spare knapsacks and stuffed it with all the chocolate and candies I could put into it. There was more than could be held in a single small knapsack, so I put the overflow into a second knapsack. That included all I had of the deluxe cocoa mix that the girls liked, plus the imported chocolate biscuits that Dixon liked. He deserved something for that classified data he had sent me.

The next task was to deal with the computers, so it was downstairs to grab some data keys and set everything up to copy. Rather than making written labels on the small data keys housings, I wrapped them with coloured duct tape to indicate their general contents. Black for videos and pics, red for the plague data and results of my analysis, blue for personal stuff, and multiple copies of each.

While those were copying, I called up the security programs and reviewed them. Actually, setting the system for my long-term absence was really no different from the settings used whenever I left the house, so that was easy to do. The only thing new was to copy out all the pass codes, including the emergency codes used whenever the pass codes were entered incorrectly and the system threatened to self-destruct. It wouldn't, but it looked and sounded damned impressive. I emailed that out to Stan and Lee. Also let them know that I was going to leave a few purely mechanical defences inside the house. They had to make sure not to smash any glass containers on the floor, and watch for spiky things. I wasn't sure that they would know what caltrops were. Kids these days don't always get a proper education.

When the first set of backups finished I pulled out those data keys, put in the next set, and started those filling up. While waiting, I did a quick scan of my email. The only one of importance was from Lee wishing me good luck, and nagging me to take my smart phone and check it along the way. Sigh. Like I would have forgotten that, silly bunny.

When all the backups signalled completion, I put the finished sets into separate pockets. That reminded me to put on my work vest before I left. It was actually a fishing vest that I liked to wear because it had a lot of pockets. Better than hanging stuff off my belt, which was already full of stuff hanging off of it.

I stuffed knapsacks with printouts, and hauled them upstairs to the kitchen. While there I took the vest out of the closet, put it on, and transferred the data keys into a couple of the pockets. The vest was already stocked with a small first aid kit, small survival kit, and a couple travel packs of tissues and wet wipes.

Heading back downstairs, I grabbed the third set of backup data keys and stuffed them into another pocket. A task for later would be to hide a set somewhere in the truck. I fired off a general email to The Group saying that I'd be on my way in an hour or so, and would let them know when I left. Best to send that now in case the satellite link cut out again.

I had to lean back in the chair and scrub at my face with my hands after sending that. It made the retreat seem real—as if all the running around hadn't managed to do that. OK, you old fool, up and at 'em.

What was next on the list? Well, that would be to get the food ready to go. I usually left that sort of thing until just before leaving. However, this time I wanted everything staged and ready to be loaded all at once without any farting around. No telling how much time I might have before the werewolves showed up again.

So it was upstairs to pour all the fluids into their respective containers, toss any foodstuffs into knapsacks stacked in a more-or-less tidy pile next to the weapons. Realizing I'd forgotten my laptops, I headed downstairs again to pack up a couple of them. A lot of my collection of books and magazines was digitized and stored, so things weren't as grim as they had seemed last night.

One more thing that needed doing was to set up the computer for remote access. I could have used one of the many cloud storage services, but they'd gotten so expensive over the past few years, and damn flaky to boot, so I had set up my own. It was just a standard Linux server app, so why not, right? Seemed like a real bright idea when I had a big fat pipeline to the Internet—now, not so much.

I checked the server and it seemed fine. So I sent an email to Lee and Stan letting them know about it, what the passwords were, and suggested they start downloading right away. Just in case.

I looked around at everything one last time. All systems were set to go and would continue to run as long as the solar array could keep the batteries charged. Since I could issue the final security system commands from the barn, I walked out and turned off the lights behind me. I didn't bother looking back as I climbed upstairs.

Oh, dear. I'd forgotten something important—my wallet with drivers licence, credit cards, and cash. It had been so long since I'd used any of that stuff that I'd quite gotten out of the habit. Thinking of cash caused me to recall that I had some stashed down in the basement. I went back down, opened up the small safe, grabbed all the cash there plus my passport. It was a bit out of date, though should suffice for extra identification.

Stuffing all that into the pockets of my vest, I closed the safe and turned to go back upstairs. A sudden wave of weariness forced me to pause for a few seconds with a hand against a wall for support. I'd been pushing myself too hard, but there was nothing I could do about that. Needs must when the devil drives, and all that.

On further consideration, maybe it couldn't hurt to have a bit of insurance. I walked over to a locked storage cabinet and opened it up. In there were the more hard-core medical supplies, like needles and sutures and strong drugs. The drugs included antibiotics, antivirals, sleeping pills, stay-awake pills, and go-pills. Despite an aversion to taking drugs, it made sense to take along something that could help me stay awake. I debated about taking the other supplies. Many of them were, strictly speaking, not something that non-medical personnel were supposed to have. Much of it was already kitted up in medical bags suitable for, say, an expedition. After a brief hesitation, I grabbed those and hauled them out. I also slipped some small vials of antacid and headache pills into the loops in my belt. Those loops were designed for bullets, but I typically used them to hold small tools.

With no more tasks left to do in the basement I took my last load upstairs, turning off the lights as I left.

★ ★ ★

Entering the kitchen, I put the medical bags next to the others and looked around. Aside from clothes, everything else was in the barn, so I went upstairs to my bedroom to pack. I decided to put things into several backpacks rather than one big pack—easier to find places to stuff 'em in a crowded truck. Inspiration struck at the last minute—toilet paper and toothpaste. Two things that you really don't want to run out of. Besides, the toilet paper would make useful padding in the truck.

After one last trip upstairs for blankets and a couple of my ergonomic pillows, I'd finished assembling my personal gear. After that I forced myself to take a ten-minute break for water and a snack before continuing. There were a couple of freezers of food in the basement and a couple more in the barn. I'd decided to take stuff from the barn freezers, mainly because the thought of hauling anything else up those damned stairs was simply beyond me. I was getting way too old for that sort of nonsense.

It was time to head out to the barn and start getting serious about all this. I figured I'd load up the truck with what I could from the barn, attach the V-plow, then back the truck up to the house and finish loading. I could only hope that the werewolves stayed away for just a little while longer.

It had occurred to me to send out the UAV to scout around before I left, and the thought did rather appeal to me. Unfortunately, there were some serious problems with that. First of all, it would take more time than I was willing to spare. Secondly, even if something made me turn back, a personal reconnoitre of the situation would be invaluable. My third, and most pressing, reason was that I didn't want to alert the Priests if I could possible avoid it.

The security system showed that all was clear, so I headed out to the barn and reached it with no problem. I gathered up all the supplies I needed from there and staged them alongside the truck without blocking its exit. I went up to the sniper nest and took a good look around without seeing anything of note. Gathering up the hunting rifle and its ammunition, I hung the binoculars around my neck and headed downstairs. After setting that load off to one side, I went to the armoury locker and selected two shotguns for the trip plus boxes of ammunition, and put them alongside the rifle.

It was time to load up the truck.

Opening up both garage doors—something I'd not done in a long time—I drove the truck just outside, stopped, and left it idling. Climbing out, I covered the rear bed with a layer of plastic sheeting. With that done, I started up the tractor and used it to transfer the bodies—specimens—onto the plastic. That worked so well that I decided to use the tractor's scoop to help transfer any heavy packages, like the frozen meat that I packed around the specimens. A layer of plastic sheeting over that, followed by another layer of frozen food. I figured that would keep the damn things cool enough for the length of the trip.

The barn's inventory included a couple of sleeping bags and some rough blankets, in case I needed to spend the night there for whatever reason. I unrolled those and threw those over the frozen layers to act both as insulation and cushion for anything piled on top. Grabbing the rifles and shotguns, I slipped them into their canvas cases and put them between the blanket and sleeping bag layers—both for protection and for concealment. I gathered up the remaining boxes of ammunition and placed those around the weapons.

Deciding to throw caution to the winds, I tossed in an extra revolver and ammunition in the same fashion. The back was piled high enough that there was only room enough for the containers of food, so I shut and locked the rear hatch. There was no more need for the tractor, so I parked it back in the garage.

There was no telling when I was going to be back, so I left a sign on the steering wheel indicating when stabilizer had last been added to the gas in the tank. It should be usable for a month or two. Beyond that the gas would start getting awfully grotty. I exited the tractor's cab with the shotgun, and took one last look around the barn.

Oh, yeah, tools. With a sigh I slung the shotgun, and selected a few sets of tools to bring. It was a damn hard choice, but I decided to stick with the basics. One toolbox of basic handyman stuff (hammers, screwdrivers, and the like), one of specialized plumbing tools, one of specialized car repair tools, and one for general electrical work. So much great stuff to leave behind that my heart almost broke. I put those toolboxes next to the rifles.

After a moment's thought, I went back inside and grabbed a couple of gun-cleaning kits. They were fairly small and were going to be needed. After a brief hesitation I added the shotgun shell reloading kit, in case I could get some gunpowder in

Toronto. All that stuff got put in the back alongside the toolboxes.

I was almost ready to close up when I decided to bring a supply of nuts and washers and screws and such. Those were always so handy that I already had a couple of toolboxes filled with the most common assortments. Those got put in the back, with a couple of blankets on top of that layer for padding. Damn—there was too much stuff, though I couldn't see what I could reasonably leave behind.

Damn, damn, and damn again.

The only extra thing I could think of was to slide a couple of portable gas tanks into their holders on the rear of the truck. I made sure to add the locking straps to them so that no-one could simply grab one or unscrew the cap and drain them. The truck had enough gas to get to Toronto with no problem, but I had the gas so might as well take it.

The only remaining thing to do was to attach the V-plow to the front of the truck. I hauled that off the wall with the portable hoist, and hauled it to the front of the garage. Manoeuvring the truck so that the front faced into the garage, I attached the plow, and tested it to make sure that it could be raised and lowered properly.

Using some extra-strength duct tape, I attached the magnetic sweepers to each of the plow's blades, in line with the wheels. With the mechanical issues completed, I made sure to disable the air bags. Wouldn't want those to deploy if I had to use the plow to ram anything.

Everything was ready to go, so after backing out of the garage I signalled the doors to close. I didn't tear up—though I had to swallow hard a few times to get rid of the lump in my throat.

I backed the truck up until it was at the stairs leading up to the kitchen. Dropping the tailgate, I trotted up to the door, got it open, and signalled it to stay open. That hadn't been done in so long that I felt rather uneasy doing it. I grabbed the containers of the dry foodstuffs and piled them inside the truck. I even managed to create a trough so that I could still see through the rear window. I kept everything from shifting around by the use of straps attached to eye-hooks inside the truck. After shutting the tailgate, I went inside the house to start on the gear designated for loading into the cab.

It took me less than half an hour to fill up the crew cab and the passenger seat of the truck. The only thing left to load was the food, to-hand weapons, and paper maps. Sure I had map software on pretty much every electronic device, and a GPS unit on the dash. It's just that paper maps were ever so much easier. Besides, I expected to be taking all sorts of twists and turns on my way out, and those units were just too stupid for that sort of thing. Some of the best routes in these parts weren't included in any electronic map that I'd been able to find. All those fool things were meant for were the well-travelled areas, not the boonies.

I loaded up all the bits and pieces in the passenger side. Most of it went on the floor, with the overflow placed on the passenger seat. Straps got put across everything so that nothing would shift around. Sudden maneuvers were guaranteed to happen at some point during this trip, if only in the city. I'd swear that the drivers in Toronto got stupider every year.

Finally, everything was loaded and ready to go. The only task remaining was to scatter caltrops around the inside of the house, as well as a few containers filled with corrosive or foul-smelling fluids. After going inside I filled up the waiting jars, then spread the nastiness throughout the house. I started distribution upstairs, put some on the stairs themselves, and finished up in the living and dining rooms.

With the defences taken care of I went downstairs and sent off an email to The Group to let them know that I was on the move, with an ETA of maybe two hours if everything went well. I could see that Grant had begun downloading files from the server. It was a smart idea to grab while the connectivity was up.

I managed to leave the basement without a sigh or tear, just leaving behind a scattering of caltrops and containers of nasty fluids. "My legacy," I thought bitterly to myself, as I walked up the stairs back to the kitchen, leaving nasties in my wake.

Upon reaching the kitchen I forced myself to pause, grab a cup of water, and sit down in a chair for a minute. I was so damned tired, and wanted a nap. Just a short nap would do me a world of good. But there just wasn't time for that. The sun was up, and had been for over an hour, and it was time to hit the road. I popped a mild stimulant pill and washed it down with some water and a few bites of bread. Speaking of which, I decided to take what remained of the loaf along with me; if nothing else, I could easily pick at it while driving.

I placed the dirty mug in the sink without washing it, made one last bio-break, and it was time to go.

After scattering the remaining nasties throughout the kitchen as I exited, I shut the inner door, and finally I was outside on the porch staring at the closed outer door. "Goodbye, Home," I whispered. "I'll try to make it back someday. You have my word of honour."

With that, I trotted down to the truck, unlocked it, and got in. After signalling the security system to enter the "I'm going away for a while" mode, I lowered the plow to just graze the ground, and headed out slowly. Reaching the end of the driveway, I turned left and headed down the road. There was a rise about a kilometre ahead, and I wanted to go slow until I knew what was on the other side.

I got to the top of the rise and slowed to a stop. It all looked so peaceful right now. Suddenly, I caught a flash of movement, and saw a werewolf darting amongst the brush.

Fucking werewolves.

Raising the plow up a couple of centimetres so it would clear the road, I gradually accelerated until I reached fifty. That seemed like a reasonable speed, all things considered. Easy to come to a stop quickly, or ram through something if it came to that.

I was on my way, with ten kilometres to go until reaching a major road that headed south.

CHAPTER SIXTEEN
Going Down the Road

I cruised along the road at a steady pace, keeping a careful watch for any problems. If it weren't for the fact that I was running from my life from a bloodthirsty horror, it would have been quite a pleasant trip. There were a few clouds gathering in the sky, with some dark ones to the south. Right now, though, the sun was shining and everything looked lovely and peaceful.

That illusion was shattered now and again by the sight of a werewolf dashing through the fields or peering at me from the safety of a wood lot. I thought I could hear the odd howl or yapping. It was hard to tell for sure over the road noise. I had not seen another car on the road, which wasn't too unusual but still unsettling.

It was only a couple of kilometres to the turnoff and there was a rise coming up that would allow me to get a better view of what was coming up. I went up the hill then slowed to a halt at the top. From that vantage point I looked down at the intersection not far ahead, and saw a pileup of cars. There was a lot of brown-red smearing, and a few small piles of ... I wasn't sure what, and didn't really want to see it close up.

It looked like it was time to take one of the alternate routes—a lesser-used side road that forked off just before the main road. With some dipsy doodling around the back roads, I could eventually get to where I needed to go.

Accelerating gradually, I hung a right at the side road. It was a rougher sort of gravel road, forcing me to raise the plow up another couple of centimetres so it wouldn't scrape. That worked well enough that I could maintain a speed of forty down the road. About ten minutes later I came to an intersection and slowed to make the left. After making the turn I kept it slow because there was a sharp right about a hundred metres up ahead, just past a dense clump of trees.

I reached the trees, hung right, and was preparing to speed up a bit when several werewolves darted out from cover and onto the road. My first instinct was to slow down, and my foot moved to the brake pedal. Then remembering the other cars, I pressed the accelerator instead. The V-plow worked perfectly as it rammed their group and flung them to either side of the road. The truck barely slowed down as it hit them, and when I glanced in the side mirrors as I sped away none of the vermin were getting back up.

Well, that had certainly worked well. I knew it would, but it's always pleasing when reality met expectations. Especially when one's expectations included survival.

Forcing my breathing to calmness, I carried on down the road. This wasn't going to be my first skirmish, and I needed to stay sharp in case there were any others. There were bound to be. Of that I had no doubt.

Then above the road noise I heard a faint series of sharp barks. Probably a lookout informing the others of the failed roadblock attempt. With an effort I kept my speed at forty, the maximum safe speed for manoeuvring on these gravel roads. Excessive speed wasn't going to help me to get out of this area as quickly as possible. Winter driving had taught me that much.

The wisdom of that bore fruit when I got to the next intersection and began to turn left, and found a car on its side blocking the road. I flung the truck into a hard right turn onto another side road and away from the blockage. This wasn't too bad, as there was road I could take about a kilometre ahead that should get me back on course.

Upon reaching that road, I had just turned left onto it when a group of werewolves jumped out of the ditches and ran towards me, blocking my path. Again I accelerated through them. Then up ahead I saw two more groups leap onto the road from the ditch. I kept my foot on the accelerator to maintain speed as I rammed through them all.

I was now just about at the limits of my knowledge of the roads around here. For the most part these small back roads criss-crossed the area and one could eventually get to where one needed to go. Unless one got onto a dead-end road, of which there were a reasonable number. Worse, one couldn't always tell a dead-end road from a through road just by the quality of the surface. The dead-enders were typically meant to go to farms, and if the farm owner had the proper political connections, then he would get a damned fine road surface courtesy of the taxpayers.

I was fairly sure that I could get to where I needed to be without hitting a dead-ender, but couldn't be positive. The road up ahead looked like a through road, so I hung a sharp left and carried on for a few hundred metres when the road suddenly swerved and I found myself heading towards a farmhouse. I slowed down as I approached and looked for a way to turn around without having to stop. As was typical for these homes, the best way to do that was to get closer to the house, and turn on the wide turnaround areas behind them.

Everything seemed fine until I got got closer. On the rear of the house there were brown-red stains on the walls and ground. I turned around as soon as I could and headed back down the road. A handful of werewolves come bounding out of the house and chased after me. Stupid, even for a werewolf.

I retraced my route, and made a left where I had initially turned right. Not my preferred route, since it took me in the opposite direction I needed to go. Still, I would rather not test my ability to ram through an overturned car. That was something to try only if necessary.

There was another road about a kilometre down and, hoping that it was a through road, I turned onto it. Wonder of wonders, it was. It even opened up into a reasonably major side road—which was an auspicious sign, I hoped. All I needed was another route to the local highway, and from there down to the local cross-highway and onto Highway 400. With any luck, from there it would be smooth sailing all the way to Toronto.

My sense of direction was modest at the best of times, and these were not the best of times. I had a rough idea of where I was going, though. Between losing track of where I was and avoiding werewolf blockades, I had to keep going south instead of over to the local highway. I finally got on a side road that had a sign pointing towards the cross-highway. Good luck—or, rather, masterful off-the-cuff navigating. Yeah, it was pure skill. Sure.

The road had some twists and curves to it, but I sailed through those with aplomb. Soon I was one sharp turn away from my goal. Making the turn, I looked ahead and saw the highway. I also saw that the road ahead was blocked by a couple of cars and a hoard of werewolves.

Damn damn damn.

Well, this was crunch time. The gap between the cars looked almost wide enough for the truck. Maybe wide enough that a nudge from the plow would let me squeeze through. The question was, would I be able to force my way through without getting stuck? And was there something on the other side that I couldn't yet see? I slowed down to gather my thoughts. The werewolves took that as a signal to attack. Yeah, of course they would. Any sign of weakness was attacked.

I took a deep breath and let it out explosively, then slowly accelerated. Now, how fast should I be going to ram through those cars? As fast as possible, or slowly and gently force things apart? Ugh—I had always hated word problems in my physics courses.

Too fast was bad—that would damage the truck. On the other hand, it was a beefy pickup, designed to take a certain amount of punishment. I was mere seconds away, so decided to split the difference. Keeping my speed at twenty until just before the cars, I slammed down the accelerator to ensure that I'd maintain velocity after impact. By this time the werewolves were throwing themselves at the truck. Some managed to hang on at various points, and some even got on the bumpers.

Then I hit square in the middle of the gap with an almighty *WHOMP*. I was bounced forward both by the force of the impact and the fact that I was slowing down because my foot had slipped off the accelerator. I let out a yell and jammed the accelerator down. With a scream of metal the truck dragged itself through. Finally I was on the other side accelerating at a fearsome rate. To either side I caught glimpses of cars in the ditches. Then they were all behind me.

There was a curved ramp onto the highway, forcing me to ease up on the accelerator. That wasn't enough, so I tapped the brakes. Actually not so much a "tap" as a "stomp", as it turned out. A fortuitous happenstance—I saw a couple of werewolves go flying forward and roll off into the ditches as I turned onto the ramp. Then I was on the highway itself.

According to a sign, Highway 400 was twenty kilometres ahead. The speed limit was eighty but I'll admit that I exceeded that by a hair. A thick hair.

It didn't take me long to get to the ramp for the 400, and I took it at the posted limit. There's a time and place to ignore the rules. Making sharp curves in a heavily-laden pickup was not that time. Then I was on the 400 itself, and heading south.

"Toronto, here I come," I muttered.

Hopefully not out of the frying pan and into the fire.

CHAPTER SEVENTEEN
Faint Hope

I drove through the rain towards Toronto. Once the adrenaline rush of escape had worn off, I was left feeling empty. Fragments of remembrances kept popping into my mind. Despite my efforts, I became awash in a maelstrom of "what if" and "maybe" recriminations. It was becoming difficult to focus. Gradually the rain washed away those tortuous thoughts. Or at least to the point where I could tamp them down and regain control of myself.

Toronto, and safety, lay ahead of me.

I had uncovered some answers, but those led to still more questions. Why were the werewolves on a mass killing spree? Why were they herding those women, and where were they taking them? Why were the werewolves absent from Toronto, yet so terribly active in the rural areas outside of the city? Why leave Toronto alone?

The answer to the last question was suddenly obvious. Because they didn't have to attack it. It was a hard target, and as such would be very difficult to take. Much better tactics would be to create a false sense of safety, take control the area surrounding it, then lay siege to the city itself. No modern city was capable of handling a siege of any duration. The werewolves would easily control Toronto within a month, if not less. But the "why" remained as much a mystery as ever. None of it made any sense.

The only chance I had to unravel the mystery of the Change

Plagues lay in Toronto. Hell was coming, and the world was slowly coming apart around us. I had little in the way of a plan, other than to contact my friends and warn them about what was coming. They had training and contacts that would be invaluable. Together we'd figure out something.

Old friends and a fresh start awaited me.

Whatever evil lay behind all this was in for a fight.

About The Author

Brian retired from the software development rat race to take up the carefree life of an author. He lives with his wife and two cats in Ontario, Canada.

For the latest news about this and forthcoming books, the occasional commentary on life, or to leave a comment (we love feedback), check out Brian's blog at

www.BrianGreiner.ca

Books by Brian Greiner

All books are available as e-books and paperbacks from :

> kobobooks.com
> amazon.ca
> amazon.com

The Ascending Darkness series
        #1   Darkness Creeps Forth
        #2   Darkness Comes Reaping

The Accursed North series
        #1 The Werewolves of Winter
        #2 The Final Doom

Darkness Creeps Forth

A terrorist attack that leaves Toronto's financial district in shambles and the country's economy vulnerable. An investigative reporter who uncovers a major national scandal and then dies of apparent natural causes before his story can be published. Investigating these seemingly unrelated events draws small-time private investigator Yancey Franklin and his friends into a century-old web of corruption and deceit that threatens the security and independence of Canada. In a desperate race against time, Yancey and his friends rush to prevent an attack by a ruthless opponent on an ageing secret military facility in northern Ontario that holds a deadly secret.

Darkness Comes Reaping

Small-time investigator Yancey Franklin has thwarted the plans of a ruthless enemy to unleash biochemical weapons in Northern Ontario. Now he is on the run and trying to uncover the secrets behind a century-old web of corruption and deceit that strives to eliminate Canada as an independent nation. In a desperate race against time, Yancey and his friends struggle to stay alive as they rush to stop their enemy's latest plan – the deadly "Harvest of Souls".

The Werewolves of Winter

The werewolves were created by the Change Plague—the result of ill-considered biotechnology. It was only their annual winter die-off that saved humanity. But every spring the Change Plague returned to create a new and more deadly crop of werewolves.

People adapted and managed to carry on despite the increasingly precarious situation.

One man, trapped on his farm north of Toronto, began to piece together hints of a deeper and more dangerous threat. With werewolves closing in, time was running out in a desperate race to uncover answers.

A novel of modern horrors, ancient prophesies, data analysis, and nerds who save the world.

The Final Doom

Felix Kurtsius discovered that the Change Plague was being dispersed as part of a deliberate attack. Toronto appeared to be the epicentre for the infection, which targeted Canada preferentially. He escaped to Toronto after werewolves began purging the rural areas of humans, only to discover insidious forces at work. In a race against the clock, Felix and his friends must use all their skills to unravel the forces behind the werewolves, and prevent the destruction of humanity.

A novel of modern horrors, ancient prophesies, data analysis, and nerds who save the world.

Preview – Darkness Creeps Forth

Book 1 in the **Ascending Darkness** series.

The Doll S7H heavy equipment trailer rumbled heavily down Highway 401. Its load was carefully obscured with padding to disguise the shape, and with tarps to protect it during transport. Nothing, however, could disguise the HET but it looked similar enough to normal low-slung transports that it would not excite any interest to any but the most discerning observer.

Secrecy was the watchword for this trip. It began at CFB Petawawa and was to end at a heavy equipment shop in Quebec. The route was not the most direct of routes, but that, too, was part of the security plan. Designed by experts and approved at the highest levels, the plan for transportation of the cargo was considered flawless. It was vital that security be perfect, to avoid any political fallout. The Minister of Defence herself was adamant that no protest groups learn of the cargo much less the route.

The cargo in question was an enhanced 2A6M Leopard tank. An excellent tank, proven in battle, it was en route from testing by the Royal Canadian Dragoons. Rightly or wrongly, the tank had become a symbol for wasteful military spending by a government committed to overspending on big-ticket military items. With the purchase of a new fighter aircraft to replace the ageing CF-18 bogged down with years of infighting and accusations of corruption, and the navy ship program grinding to a halt due to incompetent management, the Leopard tank upgrade program was the latest big-ticket item to come to public attention. To buy votes in Quebec, the government had ignored qualified firms in Western and Central Canada to give the upgrade order to an inexperienced firm in Quebec. Protesters of all stripes, from anti-war activists to budget waste protesters to anti-Quebec protesters to people just fed up with the whole venal collection of toadies and self-serving mercenaries in Ottawa, had zoomed in on this latest scandal-ridden boondoggle for all sorts of reasons. Oh, and national security played a small role in the security concerns, but only to the professionals. The politicians and bureaucrats were only worried about the protesters and political spin. Because of the overwhelming need not to draw attention to the trip the HET travelled alone with no escort, in the wee hours of the early morning to avoid traffic.

As the HET approached Highway 427, it suddenly signalled a lane change. It continued changing lanes until it was heading south on the 427. Surprisingly, this did not elicit any comment from Security Control who was monitoring the progress of the HET via a wireless communications link from the on-board GPS. This was, perhaps, not so surprising since the GPS and associated data link were actually on board a van that had been pacing the HET and was continuing eastward along Highway 401.

Soon the 427 came to an end and the HET continued eastward along the Gardiner Expressway. The HET was not seen as out of place, since with all the construction occurring such a transport was a common sight as they hauled large bulldozers and such from site to site.

As the HET approached downtown Toronto it began to gradually slow down, letting the sparse traffic pass it. Eventually it came to the Harbour Street exit, and it finally came to a stop with its flashers and tail lights strobing rapidly. A half-dozen men poured out of the cab and began slashing at the lines holding down the tarps, which were rapidly pulled off to reveal the Leopard within.

Suddenly, with a roar, the Leopard tank erupted into life. It spent a few seconds bellowing curses at the sky, then rolled off the HET and onto the roadway. From there, it accelerated down the ramp and onto Harbour Street. Picking up speed it turned north on Bay Street. Smoke began belching from the sides of the turret, and the *wumph* of the side-mounted mortars was heard at regular intervals.

A police car on a side street roared up with sirens blazing, but was quickly silenced by bursts from the 7.62mm machine guns.

As the tank passed Front Street, suddenly the main 120mm smooth-bore gun vomited with a roar of smoke and sound, and a split-second later the side of a building exploded into the night. Then another roar from the main gun and another building exploded. The main turret swung from side to side, periodically spewing destruction. The machine guns added a background chatter to the main gun, clawing away at buildings and vehicles.

Thundering past Wellington Street, King Street, Adelaide Street the guns of the tank raked destruction along either side of its path.

Onward past Richmond Street, then on Queen Street it slowed slightly as it jogged left then right and drove onto Nathan Phillips Square in front of City Hall. The tank fired one last blaze of destruction into the middle of City Hall, then fell silent.

A brightly-coloured orange helicopter noisily clawed its way from the sky and landed in the Square, off to one side of the tank.

The top of the turret opened up and out came the black-clad crew of the tank. They scurried into the waiting helicopter and were whisked into the night. A fountain of flame erupted from the tank as the incendiary charges left inside ignited. An answering eruption of flame answered from the Gardiner Expressway as the HET burned as a result of similar charges.

The helicopter made a powerful leap upwards and made a quick flip to fly south as it rapidly gained altitude to rise above the smoke and haze of the destruction wrought by the tank. It continued flying south until it got to the lake shore, then banked, flew down towards the water, and was lost in the waiting darkness.

The city was silent for a moment.

Then the screams of broken buildings and broken flesh split the early morning darkness.

Preview - **Darkness Comes Reaping**

Book 2 in the **Ascending Darkness** series.

It was the sound that got his attention when awareness returned to him. A soft meaty thudding that sounded vaguely familiar. Then came the feeling of a sharp twisting movement. It puzzled him at first, then he realized that the former always seemed to precede the latter. Following the movement came a sensation of pressure, building quickly to a dull pain that spread from the point where the pressure had occurred. He fit the pieces together and realized that all of the events were related, somehow, and the process of figuring it out gave him a vague sense of accomplishment. After some indeterminate time the process was repeated. Then again. And again. It gradually occurred to him that not only were all of the event related, but that they were happening to him. Something was hitting him. He tried to think, but the sounds and motion of the repeated blows made it impossible to hold together a chain of coherent reasoning. And he was tired. So tired.

The various sensations stopped, finally, and he felt grateful for the quiet and a chance for his thoughts to coalesce into something vaguely coherent. He became aware that something new was happening, something trying to get his attention. Voices. That was what they were, voices that saying something. He tried to focus his shattered attention on what they were saying - maybe it was important. Everything felt so thick to him, thick and disconnected.

"Mister Franklin" he heard the voice say, over and over again.

This confused him. He didn't know anyone named 'Mister'.

The voice continued its chanting, in a slow melodic manner.

He finally came to the realization that the voice was talking to *him*. With this realization came a limited return of awareness. He had a body, with a head and torso and arms and legs. He had forgotten about them, somehow. And he was lying horizontally on a hard surface, unable to move his arms or legs. The trickle of awareness increased, and memories started coming back to him. Memories of imprisonment and beatings. He was being beaten. Again. But he couldn't remember why. Everything hurt, and he was so tired.

"Mister Franklin" the voice intoned, "The Fist of Tolerance takes no pleasure in these activities. We only seek to guide you to The Path, but we require your assistance. Please, we beg of you, help us to guide you."

Yancey carefully shook his head as if to clear it, and opened his eyes as much as the swollen flesh surrounding them would allow. The bright light cut like a knife, and he quickly shut his eyes again and tried to move his head away. Strong hands firmly held his head, and a cool cloth was placed over his eyes. Yancey made a soft sigh that rustled through dry chapped lips.

"We have dimmed the lights for you, Mister Franklin" intoned the voice, "And we will try to make you comfortable, for a time. You must realize that coming to The Path is inevitable, for it is the will of God that we do so. Each and every one of us. This scourging of the flesh is necessary only because you resist the inevitable. All that is required is for you to confess. Confess and tell us everything that is in your heart. Tell us how you found this place. Tell us where your friends are. Tell us about the Shattered Palace. Confess. Confess and receive God's blessing and forgiveness. Confess and be comforted in body and soul."

Memories started to come back, like a broken mirror reassembling itself. Yancey remembered that he was in the hands of the Sword of Infinity Ascending. He remembered being captured. He remembered the interrogations. Most importantly, he remembered that his friends were now safely away from the

Sword. Nothing could force him to betray or endanger them. Nothing. He tried to form words, but his lips refused to cooperate. He felt a moist cloth against his mouth, easing the dryness. The cloth was removed and he tried again to speak. This time his lips worked, or at least well enough to form words.

"Fuck you."

Not many words, and not everything that he wanted to say to his captors, but it would suffice.

He felt the cloth around his eyes being removed, and then felt the heat of the blinding lights returning.

"You have only yourself to blame for this, Mister Franklin" said a deep sad voice, "The Fist of Tolerance exists only to guide sinners back to The Path ordained by God. You are a lost soul, and we will help guide you back to The Path. Remember that as we scourge the flesh."

The beating began again. And as before, his inquisitors were puzzled by the laughter that bubbled out of their captor's mouth before he lapsed into semi-consciousness. Yancey knew something they didn't, and the realization always made him laugh. He knew that the beatings couldn't break him. As a child he had grown up with similar sorts of beatings, and and from long practise knew how to retreat into himself to escape the pain.

Some things never change, he thought just before the kaleidescope of memories claimed him once again.

Preview - The Final Doom

Book 2 in the **Accursed North** series.

Rain washed blood off the truck as I drove down the highway, but couldn't touch the memories of the horrors I had left behind. The sight of bloody remains of people, both neighbours and strangers, continued to haunt me. The werewolves had begun to purge humans from the rural areas north of Toronto. No doubt the city would be next. I had survived the purge, but didn't know what to do other than run.

The fucking werewolves had ruined everything. Smashing through them with the truck didn't bother me, to be honest.

As I lost myself in remembrances, the wheels touched the unpaved shoulder and I struggled to fight the truck back onto the road. Losing focus was dangerous, especially given how tired I was. Speaking of which, it couldn't hurt to pop another mild stimulant—it was only my second of the day. I washed it down with some coffee from a thermos and a couple bites of bread. It all served to settle my stomach as well as my nerves.

It was a long drive to Toronto, and I couldn't afford to stop. My friends were waiting for me, and needed the new information I was bringing. Assuming one considers werewolf corpses to be "information". The werewolves were changing into something different, something deadlier than the world had been seeing these past few years. And that was in addition to their greater than normal numbers. No-one understood why.

Just before the purge, I had discovered that the Change Plague was actually a series of yearly plagues that emanated from Toronto. The how and why of that were more unknowns that needed answers. Hopefully my friends could help me figure it all out.

The rain began to let up the closer I got to Toronto. Fortunately, it had managed to do a decent job of cleaning pieces of werewolf off the plow and pickup. A pickup with a plow was odd enough at this time of year. One with blood and body bits on it was sure to attract attention.

Rolling down Highway 400, I was struck by the paucity of traffic. It was noon-ish, and so past rush hour, but it should have been busier than this on a week day. Maybe I had just got lucky and hit a break between traffic pulses. It was about time that I caught a break.

Speaking of which, the plow was bouncing up and down rather more than I would have liked. Ramming through those cars hadn't done it any good, nor had slicing through werewolves. I worried that the support struts were knocked awry or broken, and having the plow drop to the ground at the speeds I was going would be a Bad Thing for sure.

Spotting a roadside gas bar coming up, I pulled over into the exit lane. After turning into the facility, I parked as far as possible from the building, with the plow facing away from it. No point in advertising my problems.

Turning off the engine I sat there in the sudden silence. It all seemed so unreal. Here I was sitting in a gas station, cars whizzing by me, and everything seemed so normal. I had escaped an attack from the legions of Hell, and I wanted to rush out and yell at everyone to run and hide because Armageddon had arrived. Though why should they believe me? Heck, right now I was having problems believing it, and I had just escaped it.

Well, there was still work to do and problems to solve, Hell on Earth or not. I got out of the truck and walked somewhat stiffly to the front to look at the plow. There were numerous dents and scrapes all along it, the worst damage being to the edges of the wings on either side.   The edges were folded back and there were a few chunks missing. Slashes of paint of different colours were embedded into the blade. Thankfully, the little blood that remained just kind of blended in. Hopefully the rain would finish cleaning it all off before too long.

Looking along the support structure, I could see that a couple of struts were bent, and the lift mechanism on the one side was broken. A closer examination showed that the struts themselves were fine. The problem was that the main connecting bolt in the lift mechanism had sheared off somewhere along the way.

My choices were to fix it or remove it and leave the plow here. The latter was not the best of options, considering that the damage and blood might cause serious questions to be raised by the police. Besides, I was loathe to abandon an expensive piece of gear. Fixing the problem turned out to be a relatively straightforward, if profanity-laced, process that took longer than it should have.

After completing the task and putting the toolbox away, I celebrated by eating some bread and drinking coffee. That sat so well I decided to have a protein bar for extra nourishment. Sighing contentedly, I listened to the rain thrumming gently on the roof of the truck.

Soon I was feeling a little too warm, so I shrugged out of my vest and tossed it to one side. Remembering the data keys stored in there, I took a couple sets out of the vest and stashed them around the cab in different spots. After that, I just sat there for several minutes, soaking up the gentle solitude. It surely did feel relaxing.

Sitting up with a start, I shook off my lassitude. Those data keys reminded me that I had promises to keep and miles to go before I could sleep. Not to mention several werewolf corpses and assorted body bits that needed to be delivered before they degraded even further. With a sigh I resealed the coffee thermos, took a swig of cold water from another thermos, and got my sorry ass into gear.

I started the truck and prepared to leave. Then I noticed what they were charging for gas, and realized that it was actually a damn good price. It never failed to amaze me how highway gas bars often had the best prices. The truck was only down a quarter tank, but best to keep it topped up. What with the end of the world coming, and all. Of course, I paid with my credit card. If worst came to worst I wouldn't have to pay it.

I was about to pull away and continue my trek to Toronto when it occurred to me to check for cell phone service. All phone service—cell and land line—had been cut off to my house for so long that I'd simply turned my phone off to conserve battery life. Rather than calling while sitting at the gas pumps, I pulled over to the parking area again. Pulling out my phone, my fingers clumsily tapped at the touch screen. To my surprise, service was available.

Somewhat hesitantly, I dialled Lee's cell number. It had been so long since I'd actually spoken to anyone that I was bit nervous. The phone rang and rang, and finally I heard Lee's breathless voice say hello. I was so shocked that I couldn't speak until she said my name a couple of times. I snapped out of my temporary paralysis and explained that I was in a gas bar on the 400 just south of Highway 9.

Lee started to cry and said it was wonderful to hear from me. I managed to calm her down by assuring that I was all right and had a truck full of goodies, including the specimens Gail wanted, and where did she want them? She blew her nose, and said something to someone else before she started speaking to me again. She told me to use the rear entrance, and gave me the street names and the best route to get there. She assured me that it was used by trucks all the time, so my pickup shouldn't have any problems.

No problems for professional truck drivers who do it all the time, perhaps. Not so much for an old man used to driving on empty country lanes. Ah, bugger, but such was life. I assured her that I would find the way and not to worry.

Did she believe me? She did not. In fact, she insisted that I program the GPS unit while she was on the line (wasting my air time minutes) and wanted to hear the unit speak out the route. Only then was she satisfied. Kids these days.

She asked how the trip had been. I said that things were fine, and I got out fine, and I'd be there in an hour or two depending on traffic. I pointed out that Toronto drivers had been known to panic if a single raindrop hit their windshield. She laughed and wished me well, and we ended the call.

It had been damn nice to hear her voice. I sat there for a minute until my breathing steadied. And I'll admit that I wiped my eyes once or twice. Putting the phone into the seldom-used holster on the front dash, I paired it with the hands-free system, and prepared to head out.

It occurred to me, that if the cell phones were working, maybe the regular radio was as well. I'd gotten so used to the solar storms wiping out both the FM and AM stations (not that reception at the farm was ever that good) that I hadn't turned the truck's radio on. Well, that and the fact that I had been listening for werewolf howls.

I tuned to one of the Toronto all-news stations to catch one of their regular traffic reports. While listening, I pulled out onto the 400, merged with traffic, and stayed at the speed limit in the right-hand lane. It was damned seldom that anyone drove at the speed limit on the 400, of course. Still, given that it was drizzling and I was out of practise at driving in traffic, it seemed prudent.

The news was depressing, with talk about the possibility of an impending depression and trade embargoes. There was nothing about werewolves. The traffic report came on, and it proved to be interesting, if puzzling. Apparently southbound traffic volume was lighter than normal due to the unexpected fewer number of commuters. There were a few scattered reports of power failures, so perhaps the inclement weather had downed some lines.

Uhm, hadn't anyone noticed fewer cars on the roads because people were being frickin' slaughtered outside the cities? Apparently that wasn't a news item. As accustomed as I had become to the media ignoring anything outside of Toronto, this was hard to understand.

I seethed about that for some minutes until I calmed down. The analytical side of my brain kicked in and I realized that there were several possible explanations for this. Maybe the government was censoring the news. Or just maybe no-one knew about it yet. That latter possibility started to sound better and better the more I thought about it.

The purge of humans in my area was recent. The whole social system that tied us all together was already strained to the breaking point and getting kind of frayed. Small OPP detachments in the boonies that didn't report in on time were no longer much of an issue. Nor were small towns that hadn't been heard from in a while. Give it a few more days and, yes, questions would start to be asked.

Toronto had always been insular and the past few years had made it more so. Everyone was more insular, in fact, keeping their heads down and just trying to get by. Keeping up the pretence that nothing was wrong. Well, I couldn't argue that that wasn't a valid response. But only up to a certain point—and that point was long past.

Thinking on such matters began to give me a headache. Actually, the headache had been building in the background for a while, but I was only now truly conscious of it. In fact, it almost felt as if I might be coming down with a flu or something. On the other hand, it could very well be due to the fact that I was exhausted and on the run after barely escaping with my life. On the run with information that my friends in Toronto needed, data and insights that no-one else seemed to have. My headache was getting worse, and I began to feel rather sorry for myself.

Enough of that maudlin nonsense. It was time for me to do my own bit of pretending everything was normal, and that meant cruising music. I switched to a music station that played the classics—the old stuff by Bach and such. I'd have preferred music from the 1950's and 60's. Alas, no-one played the real classics any more. Sigh. In any event, concentrating on driving while listening music seemed to mute the headache, and made life seem sweeter. Something about that bothered me but I decided that lack of pain was better for driving, and focused on the music.

And so it was that I rolled on down the highway, reaching Steeles Avenue, then Finch, and finally the turnoff to the 401. Now came the fun part. I exited onto Highway 401 and headed east. With a minimum of slowdowns (minimum for Toronto, that is) I arrived at the 404 and headed south, and onto the Don Valley Parkway. Or Don Valley Parking Lot, as many people called it.

To my surprise traffic wasn't too bad, for Toronto. Damned scary for an old man used to driving in the country. I told myself to suck it up 'cuz the worst was yet to come. That is, when I got off the DVP and went into downtown Toronto. I had once thought of that as Hell on Earth, and even now it ranked a close second for that title.

The less said about that trip the better, I think. I followed the soothing voice of my GPS unit, and came to loathe it. Turn here, turn there, it would say. However, it didn't have to deal with onrushing traffic and idiots who honked at me. Damn punks who thought they owned the damned road. Piss on 'em. I went where I had to go, and if they wanted to waste their pretty cars on my built-like-a-brick-shithouse pickup, well that was their call, wasn't it? Fortunately none of them did, although it was a damned near thing a few times.

Eventually I got to the rear of the ROM, just like Lee had told me to, and I backed up into an empty slip in the delivery area. Turning off the engine with a heavy sigh, I rested my head on the steering wheel for a few seconds. Stifling a groan, I sat up, reached for the cell phone, and called Lee. She answered after the first ring and yelled out, "He's here," to someone.

I was wondering how to respond to that when I heard the big delivery door on the building roll up. Glancing in the side mirror I saw Lee holding up her phone and waving. I gave a small wave back, and disconnected the call. No sense in wasting air time or battery. I was about to climb out of the truck when suddenly I was confronted by a crowd of smiling faces. It was everyone in The Group.

Damn, but it warmed my heart to see them. I stumbled out of the cab and hugged and shook hands with them all. It must have been allergy season, 'cuz everyone had the sniffles, even me.